Pascal Garnier

Pascal Garnier was born in Paris in 1949. The prize-winning
author of over sixty books, he is a leading figure in contemporary
French literature, in the tradition of Georges Simenon. He died
in 2010.

The Panda Theory

The Panda Theory

Pascal Garnier

Translated from the French
by Gallic Books

Gallic Books
London

A Gallic Book

First published in France as La Théorie du panda by Zulma, 2008
Copyright © Zulma, 2008
English translation copyright © Gallic Books 2012

First published in Great Britain in 2012 by Gallic Books,
59 Ebury Street, London, SW1W 0NZ

A CIP record for this book is available from the British Library
ISBN 978-1-906040-42-0

Typeset in Fournier MT by Gallic Books
Printed and bound by CPI Group (UK) Ltd, Croydon, CR0 4YY

2 4 6 8 10 9 7 5 3 1

He was sitting alone at the end of a bench on a deserted railway platform. Above him, a tangle of metal girders merged into the gloom. It was the station of a small Breton town on a Sunday in October – a completely nondescript town, but certainly Brittany, the interior anyway. The sea was far away, its presence unimaginable. There was nothing picturesque here. A faint odour of manure hung in the air. The clock said 17.18. Head bowed, his elbows on his knees, he examined his palms. Hands always get dirty on trains, he thought. Not dirty exactly, but sticky, especially under the nails, with that grey grime that comes from others who have touched the handles, armrests and tables before you. He raised his head again, and, as if spurred by the surrounding stillness, stood up, grabbed his bag, walked a few metres back up the platform and took the underpass to the exit. No one crossed his path.

He used his teeth to tear open the plastic wrapper of the tiny tablet of soap then washed his hands thoroughly. The washbasin had two taps, which meant that he had to switch between the freezing water from the left and the scalding water from the right. He didn't intend to look in the mirror but couldn't help catching sight of himself as if he were an anonymous passer-by in the street. The waffle towel, staple of cheap hotels, was little bigger than a handkerchief. He looked around the room as he dried his hands. A table, a chair, a bed and a wardrobe containing a pillow, a moss-green tartan blanket and three clothes hangers. All made of the same imitation wood, MDF with a rosewood veneer. He flung the towel onto the brown patterned bedspread. The room was stifling. The radiator had just two settings, on and off. He had once disposed of a litter of kittens by shutting them in a shoebox lined with cotton wool soaked in ether. The miaowing and scratching had not lasted long. His bag sat at the foot of the bed like an exhausted dog, the handles flopping by its sides, the zip tongue hanging out. He yanked the curtain back and flung open the window. Still that manure smell. A streetlamp cast a pale glow over half a dozen lock-up garages with corrugated-iron doors of the same indefinable colour. Above it all, the sky, of course.

And, of course, the bed was soft. The frosted-glass lampshade overhead, clumsily suggesting some sort of flower in bloom, failed to brighten up the room. He switched it off.

'Do you know anywhere round here to have dinner?'

'On a Sunday evening? Try the Faro. It's the second left as you go down the boulevard. I don't know if they're open though. Do you want the door code in case you come back after midnight?'

'No need. I'll be back before then.'

The receptionist was called Madeleine, or so the pendant round her neck informed him. She wasn't beautiful, but not ugly either. Somewhere between the two. And very dark-haired; there was a hint of a moustache on her upper lip.

A few dark shops, like empty fish tanks, lined the street. A car passed in one direction, two in the other. There was no one on the street. The Faro was more of a bistro than a restaurant. Apart from the owner, sitting behind the counter with a pen in his mouth, engrossed in some calculation, it was empty.

'Good evening. Are you open for dinner?'

'Not tonight.'

'Ah, well, in that case I'll have a Coke. Actually, no, a beer.'

Off his stool, the man barely measured five foot four. Stocky with bushy hair, he resembled a wild boar but with doe eyes and long curling lashes. The man pulled a beer, gave the counter an automatic wipe, and placed the drink on the bar.

'I usually do food, but not tonight.'

'Too bad.'

The owner stood awkwardly for a moment, his eyes lowered, busying himself with his cloth, and then returned abruptly to his stool behind the till.

Other than the four brass lamps illuminating the bar, the rest of the bistro was in total darkness. Probably because there weren't any other customers. You could just make out the tables and chairs and, in the back room, children's toys: a pedal tractor, building blocks, Lego, an open book, sheets of paper and scattered felt tip pens.

He didn't touch his beer. Perhaps he didn't really want it.

'Were you after food?'

'Yes.'

'My wife does the cooking. But she's in hospital.'

'I'm sorry to hear that.'

For a moment, the only sound in the bar was the fizzing of the beer's froth.

'Do you like salt cod stew?'

'Yes, I think so.'

'I was about to close. There's some left, though, if you like.'

'That sounds great.'

'Well, take a seat. No, not here, come through.'

The back room erupted suddenly in a blaze of lemon-yellow fluorescent light. The two men picked their way over the pedal tractor, the building blocks, the Lego bricks and the brightly coloured children's drawings.

'You can sit there.'

He sat down at a table covered with a daisy-patterned apple-green oilcloth, facing a huge television.

'I won't be a sec,' said the owner. Before leaving the room he pressed a button on the remote. The TV screen spewed a stream of incoherent images and gurgling sounds, like blood bubbling from a slit throat.

… BUT THE FINAL DEATH TOLL IS NOT YET KNOWN. IN NORTHERN IRELAND …

'*Bacalao*!'

The owner placed two plates heaped with salt cod, potatoes, peppers and tomatoes on the table along with a bottle of *vinho verde*.

'*Bon appétit!*'

'Thank you.'

… THE PARENTS HAVE ISSUED A MESSAGE TO THE KIDNAPPERS. INTERVIEWED EARLIER …

'My wife, Marie, makes it, but I'm the one who taught her. I'm Portuguese, she's Breton. All she could cook was pancakes. She still makes them. You've got to make crêpes in Brittany! Are you a Breton?'

'No.'

'I thought not.'

'Why?'

'A Breton downs his glass in one. But you haven't.'

'Is it serious?'

'What? Not being a Breton?'

'No, your wife.'

'No, it's a cyst. She's tough. She's never been ill before. I drove her to the hospital this morning. The kids are at their grandmother's. It's best for them.'

… NO ONE WAS KILLED IN THE ACCIDENT. FROM OUR CORRESPONDENT IN CAIRO, LAURENT PÉCHU …

'How many do you have?'

'Two, a boy and a girl, Gaël and Maria, seven and five.'

… IT COULD JUST BE HUMAN ERROR …

'How about you? Do you have any children?'

'No.'

'Are you a sailor?'

'No.'

'I only ask because of your reefer jacket.'

'It's practical.'

… AT HALF-TIME, THE SCORE WAS 3–2 …

The salt cod hadn't been soaked for long enough. He didn't like the *vinho verde*. He would have preferred water, but there wasn't any on the table. He only had to ask. The owner would have given him some, like the beer he had not drunk. Stupid.

'Do you know Portugal?'

'I've been to Lisbon.'

'What a beautiful city! It's huge! I'm from Faro myself. It's also pretty, but smaller. I came to France in '77, to Saint-Étienne, as a builder. And then …'

… TRIUMPH AT THE OLYMPIA. LET'S HEAR WHAT THE FANS ARE SAYING …

'… I left the building trade to open the restaurant with Marie. Would you like coffee?'

'No, thank you.'

'Okay.'

… OVERCAST BUT WITH SUNNY SPELLS IN THE LATE AFTERNOON …

'That was very tasty. How much do I owe you?'

'Ten euros? I won't charge for the beer.'

'Thank you.'

… WONDERFUL EVENING AND STAY WITH US HERE ON CHANNEL ONE …

'I thought I'd be eating alone tonight. I'm José by the way. And you are?'

'Gabriel. See you tomorrow.'

'Yes, tomorrow, but as long as Marie is in hospital I'm not opening the restaurant.'

'That's fine.'

'Do you have a fridge?'

'Er, yes.'

'Could you put this in it until tonight?'

'What is it?'

'Meat.'

'Of course, that will be fine.'

'Thank you.'

The hint of moustache on Madeleine's lip was effaced by her warm smile as she took the five hundred grams of boned lamb shoulder. Anyone watching would have found the scene somewhat biblical. Today, Madeleine looked beautiful.

The flimsy wire hanger was designed for summer outfits and it sagged pitifully under the weight of the wet reefer jacket. It had been raining since early morning, a light rain that was perfectly in keeping with the town and gave it a certain elegance, a veneer of respectability. Gabriel had delighted in it from the moment he had opened his eyes; it was like a kind of salutary grief, an unobtrusive companion, an intimate presence.

There were people about, mothers taking their children to school and housewives weighed down by bulging shopping baskets. Mainly women. The men were digging holes in the road and replacing the rotten, rust-eaten pipes with new grey plastic ones. They seemed to revel in making a lot of noise and wheeling their big orange diggers in and out of the pus-yellow mud. It was a typical Monday. The shops showed off their best wares with the clumsy vanity of a girl getting ready for her first dance: bread, flowers, fish, funeral urns, medicines, sports equipment, houses for rent or sale, every kind of insurance, furniture, light fittings, shoes and so on.

He had tried on a pair of shoes just because the shop assistant seemed bored all alone in her pristine shop. But he had not bought them. He had apologised, saying that he was going to think about it. Not a sale, but a glimmer of hope at least. It didn't take much to make people happy.

After that he had stopped at a café for a hot chocolate and found himself sitting next to two young men in ill-fitting suits who talked business with the seriousness of a pair of children playing at being grown-ups. From what he could gather, their problem was how to get rid of two hundred pallets of babies' bottles and as many unfortunately incompatible teats.

'Africa. It's the only way …'

On leaving the café he had found himself outside the butcher's gazing longingly at a rolled shoulder of lamb garnished with a cute sprig of parsley. It made him think of baby Jesus.

The radiator continued to pump out a suffocating heat. He felt overcome by a kind of tropical fever. The bed morphed into a hammock and a mangrove swamp of memories closed in on him, incoherent, tangled.

There had been toys scattered about the empty house there as well.

'You can see, can't you, Gabriel, she had everything. EVERYTHING!'

His friend Roland made a sweeping gesture that encompassed the vacant space. It still smelt of fresh paint.

'You can't tell me we wouldn't have been happy here!'

Gabriel had not been able to think of a response. He had merely shaken his head. It was sadder to see it like this, virtually unlived in, than it would have been if a bomb had hit it. Nadine, Roland's wife, had left with the kids barely a week after moving in. Everything was achingly new. Most of the furniture was still wrapped in plastic.

'"I don't like chickens." That was her only explanation! Christ! She could have said earlier! I could have kept pigs. Or something else. You've seen the sheds, haven't you? They're a long way from the house. You can't smell them. Or hear them. A farm with two thousand chickens, the very best, state of the art! I'd have paid it all off in ten years! You've seen it, Gabriel; it's impressive, isn't it?'

He had seen it. Roland had shown him around. It was awful. He couldn't help but be reminded of a concentration camp. Two thousand albino chickens under ten metres of corrugated-

iron roofing, fluorescent lights glaring day and night, the birds clucking and tapping their beaks like demented toys. And an appalling sickly smell, which the ambient heat only made worse. He had hurried out to stop himself from throwing up. For a long time after, his eyes burnt with the apocalyptic scene.

Roland wept softly, fists clenched, his forehead pressed up against the window.

'They delivered the frame for the swing this morning. If you only knew how many times I've dreamt of the kids playing on the swing. Their laughter ... Why didn't she tell me sooner that she didn't like chickens?'

The Loiret can be pretty in the spring. The tubular structure of the swing frame stood stiffly between two clumps of hydrangeas. Gabriel had cooked a comforting blanquette de veau *for Roland. But his friend had barely touched it. He had downed glass after glass, mumbling, 'Why? Why?' over and over again.*

Two days later he heard that Roland had hanged himself from the swing frame.

Yes, there had been toys scattered there as well ...

'Do you want your meat back?'

'Yes, please.'

'Hold on, I'll go and get it.'

Two large suitcases cluttered the lobby. Someone had either just arrived or was about to leave.

'Here you are. What kind of meat is it?'

'Shoulder of lamb.'

'For a roast or stew?'

'A roast – just with onions, garlic and thyme.'

'That's the way I like it as well. Are you doing the cooking?'

'Yes, it's something I enjoy. It's for some friends.'

'You'll have to cook for me one day!'

'Yes, why not?'

'Okay then. Have a nice evening and make sure you take the door code this time. Dinners always go on till late.'

'If you say so. Goodnight, Madeleine.'

'What's that?'

'A shoulder of lamb.'

'Why are you bringing me a shoulder of lamb?'

'I was thinking of cooking it for the two of us, here, tonight.'

José's eyes widened as he looked from the bloodstained parcel of meat to the unblinking expression of his customer standing at the bar.

'That's a strange idea.'

'Is it? It's just … As I passed the butcher's this morning the meat looked good. But perhaps your wife's back from hospital?'

'No, a few more days yet.'

José seemed on edge. At the other end of the bar, two regulars had interrupted their dice game to watch them curiously.

'Do you want something to drink?'

'The usual please, a beer.'

José poured the beer then excused himself and went over to the two men by the till. They exchanged a few words in hushed voices. The men nodded their heads knowingly and resumed their game while José headed back to Gabriel, the tea towel slung over his shoulder.

'All right then.'

'Can you show me where the kitchen is?'

'Follow me.'

It was small but well equipped and very clean.

'The pots and pans are in this cupboard, the cutlery in this drawer.'

'I'll manage.'

'I'll leave you to it then.'

'No problem. It'll be ready in about half an hour. Would you prefer potatoes or beans?'

'It's up to you. Tell me, why are you doing this?'

'I don't know. It just seemed natural. You're on your own, and so am I. You don't mind, do you?'

'Not at all. It's just a bit unusual.'

The lamb had fulfilled its promise: juicy, cooked medium so it was still pink in the middle, with a crispy skin. All that was left on their plates at the end were the bits of string. The deliciously tender potato gratin had also been polished off. As he had carried the steaming, sizzling dish through from the kitchen, Gabriel had seen José sitting awkwardly at the table like an uncomfortable house guest, staring at his own puzzled reflection in the black screen of the television which he had not dared to turn on.

'Relax, make yourself at home,' Gabriel had wanted to say.

They had wolfed down their food, their grunts of satisfaction punctuated by timid smiles.

When he was full, José had leant back in his chair, his cheeks flushed.

'Now that was quite something. Bravo! You'll have to give me the recipe for Marie.'

'It's not difficult; the key thing is the quality of the ingredients.'

'Even so … Are you a chef?'

'No, but I like cooking from time to time. I enjoy it.'

'You've got a talent for it. Do you like port, by the way? I've got some vintage, the real thing. My brother-in-law sent it to me from back home. You can't buy anything like it here. They make all kinds of rubbish out of cider or *chouchen*. Tell me what you think of this.'

The toys had gone. He had not noticed before. He felt lost all of a sudden, somehow disappointed that the scattered toys were no longer there and the television silent. He felt as though he had narrowly missed something. A train perhaps? His heart was hammering in his chest as though he had been running.

'Here you go, try this!'

José poured the syrupy ruby liquid into two small glasses. It looked like blood. From the first mouthful, Gabriel felt his insides become coated in crimson velvet.

'What do you say to a bit of fado? Have you heard any Amália Rodrigues?'

'I'm not sure.'

'She's divine! Hold on …'

José leapt up and waddled bow-leggedly into the living room. A cassette player clicked into action and the heartrending sound of a voice dripping with tears rose through the gloom.

'It's wonderful, isn't it? I think it's the most beautiful sound in the world. Do you ever get homesick?'

'I don't know. I suppose so.'

'Where are you actually from?'

'I move around.'

'But you must have been born somewhere.'

'Naturally.'

Not getting anywhere, José poured himself another drink.

'It's none of my business really. I'm only asking because those are the kind of questions you ask when you're getting to know somebody.'

'True enough. What's she singing about?'

'The usual stuff: broken hearts, one person leaving, the other left behind. You know, life.'

'Do you miss your wife?'

'Yes. It's the first time we've been apart since we were married. I find it hard to sleep on my own. I couldn't last night. I cleaned the house from top to bottom, as if I was looking for her underneath the furniture. Stupid, isn't it?'

'No, not at all.'

'I went to see her this morning at the hospital, but she was asleep. The doctors told me the operation went well.'

'That's good.'

'Yes, only another two or three days to go. It was raining

this morning. It always rains here, for days and weeks at a time.'

Amália Rodrigues fell silent and, as if to confirm what José was saying, they heard raindrops pattering on the zinc roof over the courtyard at the back.

'Have you ever thought about moving back to Portugal?'

'Yes, but Marie's a Breton. To her, Portugal is a place you go on holiday. Nothing more.'

'And what about you, here in Brittany? Is it a holiday?'

'No, it's for life. The kids were born here. You know how it is.'

A car passed by in the street, like a wave sweeping through the silence.

'You're not drinking?'

'No, thank you, I'm fine. Anyway, I'd better be off.'

'It's not that late …'

'I get up early.'

'Ah, well. It's been good fun. Are you coming back tomorrow?'

'I think so.'

'I told my friends earlier, the ones playing dice, that you were one of Marie's cousins. It would have been complicated to explain.'

'Good idea.'

'So I'll see you tomorrow. And I'll cook!'

It was a cave, a modern-day gloomy concrete cave at the back of an underground car park. Many had lived there, some still did, leaving evidence of their squalid existence painted on the walls: smears of shit, obscene graffiti, markings daubed in wine, piss and vomit. Burst mattresses and soiled blankets were piled up like animal skins in a rotting heap, teeming with so many lice, crab lice and fleas that they appeared to be coming to life. The place stank, though it was worse outside, except that it was so cold there you didn't notice it. Simon's squatting silhouette stood out from the shadows like a figure in a Flemish painting. In front of him, meths fumes rose from an empty pea tin which was precariously balanced on a small gas stove. Wearing frayed mittens, he held the stove steady with one hand; with the other, he dangled a chicken over the flames by its neck.

'Couldn't the old bitch have given you a cooked one?'

'She was on her way out of the supermarket. She'd got two for one. It was still kind of her.'

'The road to hell is paved with good intentions. Do they think we've got all mod cons here? Pass me the wine.'

Beneath the scarf wrapped round his head, Simon's swollen eye was watering. He raised the bottle to his cracked lips and toothless mouth and took a long swig while keeping his eyes on the chicken that had started to char over the flames.

'It's burning.'

'Only the skin. We'll scrape it off. I'll turn it over.'

Simon grabbed the chicken by its feet and flipped it over, causing its comb to catch alight. He quickly blew it out.

'"Et la tête, et la tête, alouette, alouette …" *Light me a ciggy, will you? This is going to take for ever.'*

Gabriel lit a crooked Gitane and passed it over. He was starting to warm up, more because of the fire's glow than its heat. He took off his leaking trainers and rubbed his feet. He had lost nearly all feeling in them from all the walking he was doing. When there is nowhere to go you spend a lot of time on your feet. He swigged the wine and from beneath his layers of worn clothes he pulled out the crumpled pages of a newspaper that had been wrapped around his chest.

'What's the news?'

'They're going to ban cigarette smoking in public places.'

'Must have been a cigar smoker who dreamt that one up!'

You could never tell if Simon was crying or laughing. Either way, a dry cough shook him like a half-empty bag.

'Oh, it's all for our own good, isn't it? Talk about a bloody nanny state! No smoking, no drinking, no fat, no sugar, no sex. It's as if they don't want us to die. How nice of them! What else does it say?'

'An inventor has just come up with an indestructible fabric.

It's cold- and heat-resistant and even bulletproof. The Vatican has ordered some for the Pope.'

'Gone off the idea of heaven, has he? He's only trying to save his own skin, like any old moron. Here, can you hold the chicken a second? My hands are full.'

The bird was now black at either end. The skin was peeling off like flecks of paint from the lead pipes in the squat they had been thrown out of three days earlier.

'Apparently lead isn't too good for you either.'

'I know! I once saw a guy riddled with it in Marseille. It took five men to carry him!'

A fresh coughing fit made Simon double over. But this time he was laughing at his joke about the lead.

'Life's a killer. Especially for the poor. To live a long and healthy life you've got to live in a villa on the Riviera and be served by a white-gloved waiter. Yeah, but the sun gives you skin cancer! Turn it over or it won't cook on that side. Shit, not like that! You're going to fuck it up … Jesus, man, leave it, I'll do it.'

The stuffy air was thick with smoke, and the smell of alcohol, charred meat and stale cigarettes. Both of them were hunched over, like monkeys in a cage. Everything was blurred, shapeless. The men weren't men and the chicken wasn't a chicken. Nothing but rough sketches gone wrong, crumpled into a ball and thrown into this stinking hole. Simon held the bird by its head and feet as if holding the handlebars of a motorbike heading straight into the wall.

'Joan of Arc.'

'What about her?'

'She's the only woman I've ever loved.'

'What made you think of her? The chicken?'

'Maybe. Or the Pope, I don't know. I used to carry a picture of her around when I was a kid. I'd wank off over it in the toilets, looking at her in that tight, shiny armour with her tidy little page-boy haircut and her flag blowing in the wind. What I'd have given for a can-opener to get inside that …! Pass me the bottle and I'll tell you.'

Simon finished off the bottle and started to sway to and fro with a fixed stare, his hands wrapped round his chicken handlebars, full speed ahead.

'I once went to Rouen. Not Mecca or Lourdes like some people, but Rouen. I went and begged in the square where they burnt her at the stake. It was the most dough I'd ever made in my life – people were throwing their money at me! I got absolutely trashed that night – it was insane! Later on I was having a piss up against a wall when I saw her in front of me, stark naked, smiling at me with her arms and legs wide open. She said: "It's about time, Simon!" and I screwed her. I screwed her like I've never screwed before. Up against the fucking wall. And you can believe it or not, but the wall started swelling as if I'd knocked it up, and just when I was about to shoot my load the wall fell in on me. But it didn't hurt, not one bit. And behind the wall, behind the wall, there was—'

Gesticulating wildly as he relived the scene, Simon's elbow smashed into the gas stove. The alcohol spilt over him and he was engulfed in flames like a living torch, while the chicken took the first flight of its short life and landed on Gabriel's knees. Simon stood howling and banging his arms against his sides as if in the throes of a laughing fit. The fire took hold of him in a dazzling display of power, like a volcanic eruption.

Gabriel froze, numbed by the wine, awestruck. Simon threw himself onto the pile of mattresses and covers and rolled about until he disappeared under a thick plume of smoke. Gabriel grabbed his bag, trainers and the chicken and ran as fast as he could. When he stopped to catch his breath by the banks of the Seine, he tore away at the half-cooked chicken and wondered what could have been behind that fucking wall.

Gabriel ripped shreds off the candyfloss and let them melt slowly in his mouth.

We should eat nothing but clouds, he thought.

In front of him a merry-go-round whirled round: as it sped up an elephant, a fire engine, a white swan and a motorbike all dissolved into a kaleidoscope of colour and bright lights, punctuated by the piercing shrieks of the children above the heady music of the barrel organ. He had never seen Simon again. Had he melted away as well? He had almost forgotten what had happened in that underground car park it was so long ago. He remembered the chicken, the taste of charcoal and raw meat. His fingers felt sticky. He didn't have a handkerchief so he wiped them on the underside of the bench. The smell of chip fat and hot sugar hung in the air. Even the rain was sweet. Nobody seemed to realise. People came and went as if the sun were out, as if they were happy. As if. It was a tiny funfair with just a merry-go-round, a tombola, a shooting gallery and a sweet stall. He had stumbled upon it after crossing the bridge that straddled the river. This was the furthest he had been in the town and he felt as though he had crossed into another town entirely. When on foot you always travel further than you expect. You only realise how far you have gone when it's time to go back. Because you always have to go back.

'Romain, sit up straight! And hold on!'

The small boy wasn't listening to his mother. Not any more. He was laughing, on the brink of hysteria, and bouncing up and down on his elephant, which was charging furiously forward, driven by its own massive weight. It trampled everything in its path: the fire engine, the white swan, the screeching mother with her hands cupped around her mouth, the town hall, the post office, the station, the whole town. Its dreary revolving existence had driven the elephant mad. The child and the elephant were one, a single ball of pure energy, out of control, hurtling through space, destroying everything in their path without remorse. They knew that this moment of freedom would be brief and so they made the most of it. Nothing could stop them while they were in orbit. It was at moments like this that you could kill somebody. You could kill somebody over nothing at all, because nothing was stopping you and you were too high to think about humanity.

The merry-go-round slowed to a stop. It was over quickly. Gabriel stood up as he had got up from the bench at the station a few days earlier, with sticky hands.

'Five shots, five balloons, the prize is yours.'

The butt of the rifle was as cool and soft as Joan of Arc's skin. It was easy; all you had to do was empty your mind. Kept aloft by an electric fan, the five dancing coloured balloons exploded one by one. Load, aim, fire … load, aim, fire. It was all over in less than three minutes.

'Well done. You're a fine shot, sir!'

The stall holder resembled a badly restored china doll with her cracked make-up, bottle-blonde hair with dark roots, and thick red lipstick that had smeared onto her false teeth. Her glazed eyes, which had seen too much, were as lifeless as those of the hideous toy panda which she placed on the counter.

'Your prize!'

At the sight of the black and white animal with its outstretched arms and beaming smile, Gabriel took a step back.

'No, no thank you. It's fine.'

'Go on! You've won it, you have to take it.'

'No, I …'

'When you win something, it's yours. Give it to your children.'

'I don't have any.'

'Well, you'd better get busy! Take it, go on. What am I supposed to do with it? I'm no thief. C'mon now, stop making a fuss.'

'Well, okay then. Thank you.'

It wasn't that it was heavy – it was just difficult to carry. He didn't know how to hold it. By the ear? By the paw?

Or by wrapping his arms round the whole thing? As he walked past, people turned to stare, some smiling and others laughing outright. The cuddly toy didn't care. It continued to gaze wide-eyed at its surroundings with the same fixed happy smile, regardless of which way up it was carried. And so Gabriel arrived at the Faro encumbered by his unwanted progeny. The metal shutter was pulled down, but he could see a light on inside. He knocked several times, the panda perched on his shoulders. Finally José appeared, unsteady on his feet and looking anxious.

'Oh, it's you. I forgot, I'm sorry. In you come.'

The shutter rolled up slowly with the grating sound of rusty metal. It ground to a halt halfway up, exhausted, and Gabriel had to squeeze underneath. José looked as worn-out as Gabriel.

'Is everything okay, José?'

'Not really. What's that?'

'A panda. I won it at a shooting gallery. I thought the kids might like it.'

'That's kind of you. Come on in.'

On the table in the back room the bottle of port stood next to an empty glass. Gabriel tossed the grinning panda onto a chair as José slumped on another. Though one was in a state of bliss and the other in despair, Gabriel couldn't help but notice a resemblance between the two of them. He sat down and waited silently while José covered his face with his hands, rubbing his eyes and stubbly cheeks.

'Do you want a drink? Shit, it's empty. I'll get another.'

José didn't move though. It was as if he was stuck to his chair, which was in turn welded to the floor. The room was silent except for José's laboured nasal breathing, drawn up from the depths of his chest. Beside him, the panda, like a happy guest, sat waiting for dinner. The only thing it lacked was a napkin round its neck and a knife and fork in either paw. It was exactly the same size as José.

'How's Marie?'

'Well, you know ... It's not a cyst. They don't know what it is. She was sleeping. I mean ... she's in a coma. She looks so different, all yellow, her nose all pinched, and purple around her eyes. She's got no mouth, just a small slit with a tube coming out. And all the machines in her room make noises like televisions that haven't been tuned properly. They either don't know what's wrong with her or they just won't tell me. I didn't recognise her at first. I thought I'd got the wrong room.'

His eyes filled with tears and his nose began to run. He was drowning from the inside. Gabriel lowered his head and traced the outline of a daisy on the tablecloth with his finger. She loves me, she loves me not ...

'Have you eaten?' Gabriel asked.

'No, I'm sorry, I completely forgot about you.'

'Don't worry. You need to eat something though.'

'I'm not hungry.'

'I could rustle something up. I know where everything is. Let me help.'

'If you want. Thank you for coming. I don't really know what I'm doing at the moment. There are some bottles under the sink. Let's have a drink.'

'I'll go and get you one.'

Pasta, tomatoes, tuna, onions and olives. Gabriel

worked like a surgeon, his actions neat and precise. It was like being back at the shooting gallery. No need to think, just act. In the space of fifteen minutes the pasta bake was in the oven, he had laid the table and filled the glasses with wine. José had already emptied his twice and was staring mournfully at the panda.

'What kind of animal is it? A bear?'

'A panda.'

'It's big.'

'Yes.'

'The children love anything that's big. It reassures them. I didn't have the heart to go and see them after the hospital. I phoned them and said that everything was okay and that the four of us would be together again soon.'

'You did the right thing.'

'They didn't believe me. "Papa, your voice is all funny," they said. You can't hide anything from kids. They're cleverer than us. When I was a kid, I knew everything, well, most things. But now I don't understand a thing. What's the point of growing up? It's stupid.'

'I'll get the pasta.'

With his elbows on the table, José hoovered up his meal. The tomato sauce ran from the corners of his mouth, to his chin and down his neck. Like an ogre. Once finished, he pushed the empty plate away and burped, then wiped his mouth on his cuff.

'Jesus, that was good! You're hired. I'm not kidding. You're hired, seeing as Marie ...'

José thumped the table. The bottle and glasses went flying. The panda slumped on its shoulder. José grabbed the stuffed animal and threw his head back. All you could see was his uvula going up and down like a yo-yo.

'For God's sake, *why*!?'

He pounded the tablecloth with his fists. The panda rolled onto the floor. José collapsed forward, his forehead on the table, his arms dangling by his sides. His back began to shudder. Gabriel picked up the bottle and glasses.

'We had everything we needed to be happy. *Everything*.'

'I know.'

José looked up and wiped his nose on his sleeve. He was frowning, his mouth twisted in an ugly grimace.

'What do you know?'

'Pain.'

José screwed one eye shut and focused the other on Gabriel. He was dribbling. He was ugly. He was hurting.

'Who are you? I don't give a shit about your pain. Why aren't you telling me she's going to be okay, that everything is going to be fine, like it was before? Why are you looking at me with those doe eyes and not saying anything?'

'Because I don't know.'

'*You don't know?*'

Furious, José leapt up, his eyes bloodshot, and knocked the table over. The veins in his neck bulged, his muscles tensed. He stood there, shoulders hunched and fists clenched, ready to pounce. Gabriel didn't flinch.

'You don't know anything. You don't know anything at all! All you know is how to cook. Get lost. Fuck off. You and your fucking bear. Beat it. I never want to see you here again. Never, ever!'

The pavement gleamed as if covered with shiny sealskin. The night skies of cities are always yellow, rain or no rain. Gabriel picked up the panda and laid it on the lid of a dustbin. It sat there, confident, radiant, offering its open arms to whoever wanted to take it home.

'When they die, cats purr. Yes, it's true, I'm telling you! When I had to have mine put down she was purring ... Hang on a second ... Monsieur Gabriel, can I talk to you a moment?'

'Of course.'

Madeleine said her goodbyes to the Sonia on the other end of the phone and hung up. She was wearing a low-cut pink T-shirt, which emphasised her chest, especially when she leant forward. Her little nameplate necklace bounced from one breast to the other.

'Are you thinking of staying for much longer?'

'I don't know, perhaps a bit longer, yes.'

'It's just that your room is reserved for someone else from the fourth to the seventh. Would you mind changing rooms?'

'No, not at all. What day is it today?'

'Actually, it's the fourth.'

'Ah, well, in that case I'll go and get my things.'

'Thank you. The rooms are practically the same, you know.'

'It's no problem at all.'

'I'm putting you in number 22. It's on the next floor up.'

'Great. I'll go and get my bag.'

'One more thing. I wanted to ask you what you were doing today.'

'Nothing really. Why?'

'I'm off this afternoon and I wondered, well, whether you fancied going for a walk? It's not raining.'

Her cheeks flushed red. She should blush more often. It suited her.

'Is that too forward?'

'No, not at all. It's a great idea. Of course, I'd be glad to.'

'I finish at noon.'

'Perfect. I'll see you later then.'

It was the first time he had seen her outside work, in her entirety, standing up and not behind the desk. She was tall, as tall as he was, maybe even taller. It was a little intimidating. Even so, it was she who lowered her eyes and clutched her bag with the awkward charm of a young girl caught stepping out of the bath.

'Okay, shall we go?'

'After you.'

She opened the door as if about to plunge into the unknown and strode off down the road on her long legs in a sort of blind charge, the tail of her raincoat flapping in the wind. She talked as fast as she walked.

'I know a great Vietnamese restaurant, or Italian if you prefer. There's a very interesting models museum and a cinema, but I don't know what's on. It's a small town. There's not a lot to do, but it is pretty, especially by the banks of the—'

'I've got some calves' liver.'

'Sorry?' Madeleine stopped in her tracks. Her dark eyebrows arched so high they almost touched the roots of her hair.

'Calves' liver. I could cook it for you if you want. I have all the ingredients. Do you like calves' liver?'

'Yes, yes, I love it, but—'

'At your place. I could cook it there.'

Madeleine looked bewildered, as if she'd been plonked down in the middle of nowhere at a crossroads of identical streets. She burst out laughing.

'You're quite something, aren't you! Why not? I live nearby.'

They walked side by side at a slower pace. Madeleine didn't say a word, but shot Gabriel the occasional curious glance, followed by a disbelieving shake of her head.

'You know,' Gabriel said, 'I often end up wandering around unfamiliar towns. I like it, but it's nice to have somewhere to go.'

'Do you travel around because of your work?'

'It's not exactly work – it's a service I provide.'

'What sort of service?'

'It depends.'

'And does it take you all over?'

'Yes, all over.'

'Here we are. I live on the third floor. The one with the geranium at the window.'

The stairwell was unremarkable. It was typical of a modest 1960s building, clean, with a succession of dark-red doors distinguished from one another by nameplates and colourful doormats. Madeleine Chotard's – that's what was written on the copper nameplate: M. Chotard – was in the shape of a curled-up cat.

Cats were everywhere in the two-bed flat in all sorts of varied guises: a lamp stand, wallpaper, cushions. There were figurines in wood, bronze and porcelain of cats jumping, sleeping, arching their backs, stretching …

'The kitchen is on your left if you want to put your stuff down.'

Even more cats in the kitchen: cat salt and pepper mills, cat jugs … Gabriel put the food on the worktop next to the hob and went back into the living room to join Madeleine. The room was small, but bright and very clean. Not a single cat's hair in sight.

'Make yourself at home. Do you want a drink before you start?'

'I'd love one.'

Being at home obviously freed Madeleine from the demeanour required at work. She was comfortable with her body, most probably sporty, natural – what's known as a fine specimen. The strip of flesh visible between the bottom of her T-shirt and the belt of her skirt when she bent over to take a bottle from the cupboard was smooth and flat, not an ounce of fat.

'I haven't got a great choice. To be honest, I hardly ever

drink aperitifs – I just keep some for friends. Do you fancy a Martini?'

'Perfect!'

It was as if there were a second world underneath the smoked glass of the low coffee table, an almost aquatic parallel universe where the reflection of the hands dipping into the bowl of peanuts merged with the floral carpet.

'It's funny seeing you here,' she said.

'It was you who invited me, the other day. You suggested I cook for you.'

'I was joking.'

'Well, I took it seriously. Would you rather go to a restaurant?'

'No! It's just that it's surprising, that's all. Normally you get to know people in a public place like a café or a club …'

'A neutral place, yes. But why do you want to get to know me?'

'I don't know. Maybe because you always look a bit sad and bored.'

'You must get a lot of people like that at the hotel, travelling salesmen, loners, people passing through …'

'This is the first time! Don't think—'

'I didn't mean anything like that, believe me. I'm happy to be here. Are you hungry?'

'A little, yes.'

'Okay then, I'll get started.'

'Do you want me to show you …?'

'No, it's fine, thanks. I'll manage.'

It was as he had expected. Luckily, he'd thought of

everything. It was a typical singleton's kitchen. The fridge was practically bare and contained just a few fat-free yogurts, half an apple wrapped in cling film, some leftover rice, a half-frozen lettuce stuck to the back of the vegetable drawer and a jar of Nutella for those nights when she needed comfort. It was touching.

The new potatoes were soon bobbing up and down in the boiling water, the shallots slowly caramelising in the pan to which he added the two good-sized pieces of calves' liver drizzling them with balsamic vinegar and sprinkling a pinch of finely chopped parsley. The surrounding white ceramic tiles, unused to such aromas, blushed with pleasure. Madeleine's face appeared in the doorway, her nostrils twitching.

'Mmm, it smells nice.'

'You can sit down if you like. It's almost ready.'

The liver was cooked to perfection, the onions melted in the mouth and the potatoes, glistening with butter, were as soft as a spring morning.

'It's been a very long time since I've had calves' liver. I never think to buy it. It's delicious. And the shallots …!'

I am cooking for you because I like you. I am going to feed you. We barely know each other and yet here we are, just inches apart, where together we're going to drool over, chew and swallow the meat, vegetables and bread. Our bodies are going to share the same pleasures. The same blood will flow in our veins. Your tongue will be my tongue; your belly, my belly. It's an ancient, universal, unchanging ritual.

'… and that's why she was worried.'

'Who was?'

'My grandmother, of course.'

'Ah, yes, sorry.'

'It was just a bit of anaemia. It often happens to kids who grow too quickly. I hated that.'

'What?'

'Minced horse meat cooked in stock. I just told you. Weren't you listening?'

'Yes, yes, of course. Minced horse meat cooked in stock. It's true. It can't have been that appetising for a little girl.'

'You said it. But she thought she was doing the right thing. I was very fond of her. I'll have a bit more wine, please. Thanks, that's enough! I think I'm a little bit tipsy.'

'Did she die?'

'Yes, five years ago.'

'And your cat as well?'

'Yes. How did you know?'

'I accidentally overheard you mention it on the phone this morning.'

'It's true. Last year. She was called Mitsouko, after my perfume. She lived to be fourteen.'

'And you haven't replaced her?'

'No, but I often think about it.'

'When you have your Nutella nights?'

'Nutella nights? What do you mean?'

'Nothing. I don't know why I said that.'

'Would you like coffee?'

'Yes, please.'

The flat had already changed. It was now filled with

the smell of cooking, rather than the smell of nothing at all. Things had been moved around and the sofa cushions were creased. There was another person there. Madeleine must have been aware of it when she heard him moving around in the kitchen. Gabriel walked over to the window and raised the net curtain. It was a small, anonymous street, the sort of street you go down on the way to somewhere else. How many times had Madeleine stood by the window cuddling her cat, waiting for something to happen down below? And how many times had she drawn the curtains without witnessing anything but the slow flowering of her picture-postcard red geranium?

'Sugar?'

'No, thanks.'

'The street isn't exactly lively, is it?'

'It's a street.'

'I sometimes think it's more of a dead end. The rent is cheap, though, and it's quiet.'

'I once lived on a street like this. One day I saw a Chinese man fall from a sixth-floor window.'

'That's awful!'

'It took me a moment to realise that it was the Chinese man from the sixth floor. He flashed past. It was a beautiful day; the window was open. I didn't see what happened, but I felt it, like a large bird or a shadow passing over. And then I heard shouts. I leant out of the window to have a look and saw something lying in the middle of the road in the shape of a swastika. There was an elderly couple across the street. The woman was screaming. All the other windows opened at once. Someone yelled, "It's the

Chinese man from the sixth floor!"'

'What did you do?'

'I think I closed the window. I didn't know him that well. We'd met a few times on the stairs. A neighbour told me later that he was a bit unstable and part of a cult, something like that.'

'It must have been a weird feeling.'

'You feel a bit of a voyeur, even if it's unintentional. All day it felt as though I had something in my eye I couldn't get out, a kind of indelible subliminal image. It was quite annoying. I don't know why I'm telling you this – it's stupid.'

Gabriel regretted telling the story. The room now teemed with falling Chinese men. Madeleine was hunched over, staring into her cup, her brow furrowed. Would she ever dare open her window again? Would she let her geranium die of thirst? What if she was indeed sporty and her hobby was parachuting? He was an idiot.

'Do you do much sport, Madeleine?'

'Yes, I like swimming. I go to the pool three or four times a week. I love it. How about you?'

'Sometimes. I like swimming in lakes. It's peaceful and relaxing.'

'I'll swim anywhere, in lakes, rivers or the sea. Ever since I was little I've loved the sea. I was never scared of it. To be honest I feel more at home in the sea than on dry land. I went scuba diving in Guadeloupe a few years ago. It was incredible. Have you been to Guadeloupe?'

'Unfortunately not.'

'It's like paradise. Would you like to see some photos?'

'I'd love to!'

Madeleine's happy memories were stored in a little imitation-leather album labelled 'Holiday 2002'. She sat down next to Gabriel and opened her bible on her knees. Every photo showed white sand, coconut palms, rolling waves, a riot of flowers, a blindingly blue sky above a turquoise sea, all framing Madeleine's perfect body, sitting, lying, standing, swimming or frolicking with the clown fish. A celebration of Madeleine as God had made her.

'If you only knew how beautiful it is over there. Everything smells great, everything feels soft, everything tastes sweet ...'

'Even the sea?'

'Even the sea. Here, hold this. All I have to do is close my eyes and I'm there. Close your eyes. Can you hear the sea?'

As the album slipped onto the floor, Madeleine leant against Gabriel who shrank back into the sofa.

'I don't think it would be a good idea, Madeleine.'

'Don't you like me?'

'Yes, I do. You're very beautiful.'

'Do you think I'm a nympho?'

'Not at all. Anyway, there's nothing wrong with that.'

'Do you prefer men?'

'No, it's not that.'

'Are you ill?'

'No, not that either.'

'So why not then?'

'I don't know what to say. But what does it matter? I cooked for you.'

'So?'

'So nothing. It's just how it is. There's nothing to understand. Don't be offended. I like you a lot.'

Carefully, Gabriel extricated himself, got up and smoothed down his hair. He was as pale as a plaster saint, haggard, tired of a life that was bringing him down.

'I'm sorry. I would have liked to make you happy. Don't hold it against me; it's not your fault.'

Madeleine stared at him from the depths of the couch like a discarded rag doll, her legs and arms splayed.

'You're weird. Really weird.'

'See you tomorrow, Madeleine.'

The wardrobe took up most of the shop window. It was a beautiful piece and the owner of Obsolete Antiques must have been proud of it to display it so prominently that it overshadowed everything around it. Made of blond wood with a shiny satin finish, it was the perfect size, a classic, devoid of cumbersome ornate embellishments. Gabriel's reflection in the shop window fitted it perfectly. It was as if it had been made for him. The wardrobe's door was invitingly ajar. The perfect sarcophagus. The journey into the afterlife would be a cruise.

'Eight hundred euros you say?'

'It's solid birch. And well built. Dovetail joints. No nails or screws.'

'Edible then?'

'I'm sorry?'

'It's edible. There's no metal in it.'

'I don't understand.'

'Forget it. It's very beautiful. Thank you.'

It was a shame that Mathieu was dead. He would have liked to buy it for him. Mathieu had already eaten one, the one in which his wife had died. She had locked herself in by accident, the door closing on her, and had suffocated amongst her own furs. Mathieu had been infatuated with his wife and the grief had driven him mad. He had blamed the wardrobe and vowed to eat every last bit of it. It took him years. But bit by bit, splinter by splinter, he had eaten the entire thing. Each morning, using a penknife, he had sliced a piece off and chewed it with the single-mindedness of which only a spurned lover is capable. It had been a mahogany Louis-Philippe wardrobe. He took barely two years to finish one door.

'You know what, Gabriel, it's the fittings that are the problem. The wood itself is fine. It's the fittings that slow me down. That's what's annoying about a Louis-Philippe.'

But Mathieu's appetite for revenge eventually diminished, and even though he was loath to admit it, his hatred for the wardrobe had turned into the same all-consuming love he had felt towards his wife. He savoured the object of his resentment with a gourmet's relish.

'I boiled a corner piece in water yesterday and you know what? It tasted just like veal!'

One night Mathieu called Gabriel in tears.

'Gabriel, come over. I've finished.'

He lay on his bed, emaciated because, ever since his fatal promise, he had stopped eating anything other than mahogany, which is hardly nourishing. The only thing left of the wardrobe was the imprint of its feet on the dusty floor and the huge oblong of darker wallpaper.

'It tasted good, you know …'

Those had been his last words. His gaunt hand, lying clenched on his chest, had unfurled like a flower and a key had fallen from his palm.

It was just about the only thing that Gabriel had kept from his former life – a key that would never open, or close, another door. He always kept it on him, deep in his pocket. It matched his body temperature: burning or freezing. He told himself that one day he would give it away or even lose it and that somebody else would find it, as that is what happened to things. They passed from person to person.

It wasn't far to the Faro, the same short distance as from Madeleine's house to the antique shop. The town was so small. The café was open. José was reading the newspaper. Behind him, wedged in a corner among some bottles, was the panda, its arms outstretched. A couple sat at one of the tables. José looked up. Because of the cigarette clamped in his mouth, you couldn't tell if he was smiling or grimacing. Perhaps both. He sighed, blinked, stubbed out his cigarette and dragged himself wearily over to the counter. He hesitated then shook Gabriel's outstretched hand, holding on to it for longer than normal.

'The usual?'

'A beer, thanks.'

José's beard had grown. Apart from the panda's determined grin, the two still looked uncannily alike.

'Well, I couldn't leave it out there for the dustmen to

take away, could I? It's not doing any harm in the corner there, is it?'

'No, it's very welcoming.'

'Yes, it'll cheer up customers. It hasn't had any effect on those two though.'

José jerked his heavily stubbled chin towards the couple.

'They look half drowned. And it's not even raining.'

The man and woman sat opposite one another with their arms folded. They leant over two empty coffee cups, their foreheads nearly touching, looking like two bookends on an empty bookshelf. The man was well into his forties. His face was angular and gaunt with deep-set eyes, hollow cheeks and nostrils. His greasy hair was swept back off his face and curled on his coat collar. The woman had her back to Gabriel, but he could see a little of her face in the mirror. She looked disreputable; a dusting of white powder coated her blotches, spots and wrinkles. She resembled a cake that had been left for too long in a shop window. She seemed roughly the same age as her companion. They both had the same mouth. Fleshy, sensual blood-red bee-stung lips. They must have kissed a lot. They weren't talking. They were just watching and absorbing one another, oblivious to the world. At the man's feet sat a dented instrument case. A saxophone, perhaps?

José gave the counter a quick wipe and snapped the cloth.

'They've been here for an hour. They're not even talking to each other. Listen, I'm sorry about last night. I was drunk.'

'Don't worry about it. How's Marie?'

'The same. A green line going up and down on a screen. Oh, by the way …' José paused.

'What?'

'I'm going to see the kids tomorrow. Do you want to come along with me? I don't feel like going on my own.'

'Of course, I'd be happy to.'

'Thanks. I don't know what to say to them. They're only little. I should buy them a present as well … Excuse me. Yes, what can I get you?'

The man was sitting up, his hand raised like a schoolchild's.

'Do you have any peanuts?'

'No, I don't.'

'Oh … shame.'

Gabriel took a packet out of his pocket. He had bought two bags from a corner shop after leaving Madeleine's flat. The peanuts he'd had at hers had given him a taste for them. You should always carry a packet of peanuts around with you.

'I've got some. Here.'

'That's kind, thanks. How much do I owe you?'

'Nothing.'

'No, really, come on.'

'I've got some more, it's fine. What's in your case?'

'A saxophone.'

'Do you play?'

'No. I'm selling it.'

'Can I have a look?'

'Of course.'

The man's hands were very long and thin, like two big

white spiders. His dirty fingernails fumbled at the clasp. Inside, coiled like a snake on dark-red velvet, gleaming under the bar's lights, lay an engraved golden saxophone.

'It's a Selmer. A real one!' said the man.

'How much do you want for it?'

'Five hundred? Four fifty? Four hundred?'

'Five hundred then. I'll take it.'

The couple stared at Gabriel as he opened his wallet and spread the notes out on the table.

'There you go. Five hundred. Good evening.'

The man's Adam's apple rippled up and down his neck. He gulped like a fish out of water.

'It used to belong to my father. You've got a good deal.'

'I wouldn't know. I'm no expert.'

Gabriel went back to the bar and placed the small coffin on the counter. Behind him, out of view, the couple grasped each other's hands, basking in their good fortune. José, his elbow on the counter and the tea towel on his shoulder, rubbed his cheeks.

'Can you play the saxophone?'

'No. Do you think your children would like it?'

José didn't answer. He lit a cigarette and took a few short puffs, squinting through the smoke.

'Maybe you're just mad?'

No matter how hard he tried, his key wouldn't turn in the lock. Through the door he heard hurrying footsteps. 'Who is it?'

Gabriel took a step back. Room 12.

'Sorry, I ...'

As the door opened, the man from the café was revealed, silhouetted against a yellow glow.

'Oh, it's you! Have you changed your mind about the saxophone?'

'No, no. It's just that this used to be my room. It was habit. I made a mistake, I'm sorry.'

The man stood there in his underpants, dishevelled, a cigarette hanging from his mouth. He seemed confused by Gabriel's presence. The corridor's timer light clicked off.

'Which room are you in?' the man asked.

'Number 22 on the next floor. I'm sorry—'

'Do you want a drink?'

'No, I'm fine, thanks.'

'Come on in. We owe you one. Rita? It's the man from the café, the one who bought the saxophone. He's in the same hotel as us.' The man leant forward towards Gabriel. 'She's a bit of all right, isn't she?'

The room, his room, stank of alcohol, cigarettes and medication. The window was closed and the radiator was on full. The woman sprawled on the bed wearing very little, her legs spread and her hands behind her head, shamelessly showing off her hairy armpits. She resembled a piece of meat lying on a cloth ready to be sliced up, Gabriel thought. Sleepily, the woman looked up at Gabriel. She seemed almost as bleary-eyed as her partner.

'Well, shit, it's a small world, isn't it?' she said. 'Sit down. We don't do standing up.'

Gabriel sat down at the foot of the bed on the room's only chair while the man poured him a mouthful of gin in a toothglass.

'Apparently, when you drink from someone else's glass you see their thoughts. Bad luck for you!'

'Thank you.'

The man rejoined the woman on the bed, his back propped against the wall. He was obviously not used to making pleasantries, but he said, 'It's not everyone who would do what you did! You really got us out of a hole you know.'

'No, I didn't know. But I'm happy to have been of some help.'

'We were broke.'

'It happens sometimes.'

'More often than we'd like! What brings you here? Are you passing through?'

'Yes.'

'Lucky you. I spent my entire childhood here. The only good thing about this shitty town is it encourages you to move on as soon as possible!'

'But you're back.'

'Forced to come back. My father. Family stuff. Money, you know.'

The man emptied his glass and handed it to Rita, who, with what looked like a huge effort, extricated herself with a sigh from the tangle of sheets and went to fill it up again. Her hip brushed Gabriel's shoulder on her way past. It was she who gave off that smell of medication, sweat and disease. She drank half the glass and then slumped back down next to the man. She kept scratching herself, on her nose and her arms. Her nails left long red scratch marks on her pale skin. Gabriel felt as though he was on a hospital visit. Just to be polite, he took a tiny sip of gin. It was lukewarm and tasted medicinal. He set it down on the table and tried to work out the best way to leave as soon as possible. But the man started up again, more for his sake than his visitor's.

'A sodding saxophone. That's all I could get out of the old bastard. This time I really thought he was done for, no fucking chance though! He's like a tick hanging on to his shitty life. A bag of decaying organs, that's all he is. But with a heart like a Swiss watch, indestructible. Tick tock, tick tock. The old fucker. He knows full well I'm up to my neck in shit and that all he has to do is sign a rotten piece of paper to get me out of it. But no! He enjoys having me on a leash like this. It's the only thing which gives him a hard-on,' the man said. 'Do you have any family?'

'No.'

'Well, you don't know how lucky you are! All my life, he's been a pain in the neck! You can smell how this town stinks, but, I tell you, it's not the manure, it's him! Yeah, him! Jesus Christ, I'm not going to settle for just the sax! No way! I don't know what the hell it was doing there. I'd never seen it before. It was in front of the door next to the umbrella stand. So I just took it. Sometimes you do things without knowing why. So as not to leave with nothing ...'

Somewhere in the far distance a clock struck eleven, the noise muffled by the dark of the night. Gabriel stood up.

'Well, it's late. I'll be on my way. Thanks for the drink.'

'I'll see you out.'

Before opening the door, the man whispered to Gabriel, 'What do you think of Rita?'

'Well, uh ... I hardly know her.'

'Physically?'

'She's, erm, well endowed.'

'Well endowed?'

'Attractive then.'

'Because I could always ... if you want ... I could go for a wander. You know what I'm saying?'

'That's kind but no. I'm up early tomorrow.'

'Ah, another time then perhaps?'

'Perhaps. Goodnight.'

José's car smelt of wet blankets, grease and stale cigarettes. As Gabriel got in, José asked him to ignore the mess; he meant the used tissues, crumpled sweet wrappers, oily rags, old chewed pens, screws, bolts, springs, the greying remains of the stuffed toy rabbit and the set of tattered road maps.

'I haven't had time.'

With every jolt, the saxophone on the back seat knocked against a big gift-wrapped box. On either side of the road, fields of mud stretched towards the hazy horizon. The landscape felt unreal. Did Gabriel believe in it? Even the presence of a few crows failed to convince him. Gabriel had felt this way all morning. He had gone through the motions, but felt nothing. Madeleine had been in her usual place, behind reception, encased in a tight-fitting grey suit, like soft armour. She had said 'good morning', asked him if he had slept well, if he liked his new room, without ever referring to the previous afternoon. They had wished each other a good day. The pavement under his feet might as well have been a rolling walkway transporting him from his hotel to the Faro. José had shaved, combed his hair and put on a clean shirt.

'What's in the box?'

'A little kitchen on wheels for Maria. Where did you eat last night?'

'Nowhere. I went for a walk and had a few peanuts before going back to the hotel. How about you?'

'I wasn't hungry. I watched TV.'

'Watch anything good?'

'I don't know. I can't remember. I went and slept in the children's bedroom. I can't sleep in our room any more.'

'Any news from the hospital?'

'No. I'll call later. It's good that you're here. I have to speak to Marie's mother, Françoise. Would you look after the kids while I talk to her?'

'Of course.'

'She's a good woman, Françoise. And brave. She lost her husband just before Marie was born. She's always managed by herself.'

Françoise stood on her doorstep flanked by the two children. Had they been replaced by weapons then she would have made a magnificent war memorial: a Grandmother Courage draped in a charcoal-grey shawl, her chin raised high, her wiry hair tamed in a tight bun and her steely eyes challenging the futility of the human condition. How long had they been standing there in front of the door? The children timidly returned José's wave as he parked the car in front of the gate.

Everything here was strangely symmetrical. Identical squares of lawn lay either side of the gravelled driveway next to identical fruit trees and identical hydrangea bushes, which grew in front of identical grey-green stone walls. You could have folded the scene in half along a vertical line starting at the point of the roof and everything on the left would have corresponded exactly with everything on the right, square of lawn on square of lawn, tree on tree, hydrangea bush on hydrangea bush, brother on sister, half of the grandmother on the other half. The grandmother now opened her hands and released the children, who ran over and wrapped themselves round their father's legs. Gabriel followed behind, smiling at the scene – the daddy bear playing with his cubs.

'All right now, kids, careful!'

'Papa, Papa! Presents!'

Gaël, a stocky little creature with curly black hair, took after his father, while Maria, with her blonde hair, pale skin and her grandmother's bright blue eyes, had obviously inherited her looks from the maternal side. They were handsome children, clean and fresh and full of life.

'Presents! Presents!'

'Say hello to my friend Gabriel first.'

The two children went over to Gabriel and planted sugary kisses on his cheeks before falling on the presents.

'Françoise, this is my friend Gabriel.'

A firm but welcoming handshake. She had instantly assessed her son-in-law's friend. She seemed satisfied.

'Your garden is beautiful,' Gabriel said.

'It never looks its best at this time of year. It's just work, that's all. It grows all the time, especially the weeds. Come in.'

Despite her slightly brusque response, Françoise didn't mean to be unfriendly. Order and discipline were what kept her going. It was the only thing she had found to support her through a life punctuated by hurt and suffering. She wore her resignation as a retired soldier wears his medals. A brave, worthy woman, she didn't ask anything of anybody.

Roast chicken, mashed potato and an apple tart. A simple and filling meal. Throughout lunch, José did his best to appear cheerful in front of the children, but each time one of them mentioned their mother his fork trembled in his hand, and his eyes, red through lack of sleep, would appeal to Françoise and Gabriel for help.

'Okay, children. I have to speak to your grandmother. Gabriel, if you wouldn't mind …'

It was ages since he had spent time with children. He had forgotten how to speak to them. He felt awkward and clumsy, oversized … Like poor old Gulliver.

'Can you show us how to play the saxophone?'

'I think you have to blow into it and press the keys.'

Gabriel took a deep breath and blew into the saxophone, but only managed a sound like breaking wind, which sent the children into fits of giggles.

'You farted! You farted!'

They all had a go on the instrument. Gaël blew with all his might, turning bright red, but with little success.

Maria, on the other hand, managed to produce three clean notes on her first go. Gaël and Gabriel couldn't believe it and were a little put out.

'I didn't know I could play! It's easy!'

She started again. Once, twice, three times. She was good. Her brother's mood darkened.

'Okay, that's enough!' he said. 'You're playing the same thing over and over. Shall we play with the kitchen now?'

Children's disagreements, unlike those between adults, were always over in a flash. The brother and sister were soon happy organising a tea party. Gaël seemed to take a real interest, sorting out all the pieces and putting them in their proper place.

'Right, what are we going to cook?'

'Snails!'

'Okay then. Gabriel, you sit there. You're the customer. What would you like to eat?'

'Snails, please. And then a steak and chips!'

'We've run out. But we've got chicken with noodles and Gruyère.'

'That'll do nicely.'

Juliette had been the same age. Gabriel had bought a live lobster and was preparing to grill it on the barbecue. His daughter peered at the crustacean waving its pincers and wiggling its tail in the smoky air, her chin just level with the table. She looked like an elf with her little upturned nose, cherry-red mouth and almond green eyes hidden behind strands of sun-kissed and sea-sprayed hair. Both of them were in their swimsuits. It was hot, very hot. The terrace shimmered in the heat.

'Are we going to eat it?'

'Yes, it's very good.'

'It's moving.'

'When it's cooked, it'll stop moving. Careful now, I have to cut it in two.'

'Will it hurt?'

'No. It'll be so quick that it won't feel a thing.'

'How do you know?'

'I just do. Watch out now.'

He split the lobster lengthwise with a sharp decisive crack. Thick liquid trickled from the white flesh onto the chopping board. The lobster's pincers stayed open as if seizing the moment. Juliette had watched the whole thing. Clinging to the table with both hands, she hadn't blinked.

'Well done!'

And then she had danced round the hot white terrace singing at the top of her voice, 'Well done, well done, well done!'

He had given her the biggest piece.

'Here are your snails, sir. Watch out, they're hot.'

Gabriel pretended to taste the blobs of playdough on the small yellow plate handed to him by Gaël.

'Mmm, they're delicious! My compliments to the chef!'

'That's me, not her.'

'Well done to you both.'

Gaël shifted from foot to foot with a tea towel over his shoulder. He looked just like his father behind the counter at the Faro. He sat down cross-legged in front of Gabriel and looked him straight in the eyes.

'Why do we only eat dead things?'

'Because … because they cook better.'

'So when Maman dies, are we going to cook her?'

Maria had picked up the saxophone again. A fourth note rose from under her fingers. She looked astonished.

'What are you talking about, Gaël?'

'Nothing. I just wanted to know. Do you want your chicken now?'

'The doctor told me he was going to try something. I didn't really understand what. Apparently, it sometimes works.'

José unthinkingly tapped the image of the Virgin Mary stuck to the dashboard, as others might touch wood. The windscreen wipers did their job, but without enthusiasm. Here it was always the rain that won.

'Your kids are very nice.'

'Yes, they're very nice. And Françoise too. And you. And Marie. Jesus! Why!'

José smashed his fist against the steering wheel. The car swerved. A red lorry coming the other way veered out of their path in a cacophony of beeping. José pulled over and collapsed over the steering wheel, his back shaking with sobs. A tidal wave of tears. What could mop up so much sorrow? Gabriel put his hand on José's shoulder. It was all he could do. He thought back to the red lorry that had been heading straight for them. He hadn't been scared. He was ready. He had been ready for a long time.

'I'm sorry, Gabriel. I almost ran us off the road back there.'

'It's okay. It's okay.'

We've already spun off the road, floundering and sinking, endlessly bailing out water.

'Would you like me to drive?'

'Yes, please. I'm a wreck.'

The town unfolded before them through the rain like a Japanese paper flower. It shone, unfurling into the most unlikely shapes, spreading out like an ink stain on a sheet of blotting paper.

For the panda everything was for the best in the best of all possible worlds. It was as happy to see the two men return as it had been to see them leave. It's only trick was to keep its arms open. It held nothing and retained nothing. Take it or leave it, it was all the same to him.

'I don't think I'm going to open.'

'Best not. Anyway, it's already late. Do you want me to make you something to eat?'

'No.'

'How about a little soup? Something small. You could have it in front of the TV.'

'Okay then.'

Leek and potato soup was the best thing for any man who was close to the edge.

'All you have to do is heat it up. I've put some butter in it.'

'Thank you.'

On the television, two football teams, the reds and the blues, battled it out. José had sunk so low on the couch he had become part of it.

'Who are you supporting?'

'I don't care. Whoever's winning.'

'Do you want me to stay?'

'No. I'd rather be by myself. Don't be offended.'

'Of course not. I understand. I'll see you tomorrow.'

'Yes, tomorrow.'

Gabriel shook José's hand. It weighed the same as a large steak.

'I was afraid you'd left.'

'I was about to.'

Madeleine looked exactly as she had done that morning, as though she had spent all day under glass, waiting for evening to come.

'What are you doing tonight? Would you like to go for a bite to eat?'

'Where? At mine?'

'No, I haven't had the time to ... What about the Chinese? Or the Italian?'

'Let's try the Chinese.'

They unconsciously fell into step together, arm in arm, left, right, left, right. They looked like an old couple. The rain fell like musical notes onto Madeleine's umbrella.

'How was your day?' she asked.

'Very strange. Do you like children?'

'Of course, well, you know, like everyone does. Why do you ask?'

'I was playing with some children today, a little boy and girl. They reminded me of stowaways on a ship. They make the most of their size and stay out of sight, but I think they want to take us over. They're clever, so very clever! When you play with them, you unwittingly collude in your own downfall. They want to take our place. I saw them the other day at the fair with their elephants, trampling everything in their way.'

'Gabriel! You can't say that! You were that age once as well.'

'But not like them. I never picked up a saxophone and played it just like that when I was five.'

'I don't understand.'

'It doesn't matter. Sorry. Ah, is this it?'

Chinese restaurants in provincial towns are always empty. The Golden Lotus was no different. There were funny rumours about what they put in their food. There were so many spelling mistakes on the menu that they used numbers to help identify what was what. Gabriel put his money on numbers 4, 22 and 16 while Madeleine went for 5, 27 and 12. The Chinese are gamblers by nature, and smile for a living.

'Tea or rosé?'

'Let's have both.'

Behind Madeleine, an illuminated waterfall flowed freely between two fluorescent pagodas to striking effect. A voice, thick with a sweet and sour accent, belonging to someone in the back of the restaurant, made Gabriel want to wave a fly swatter about. It made him think of that well-worn line from adventure films: 'It's too quiet –

something's up.' Madeleine leant over the table, her chin cupped in her hand.

'It was nice of you to take me out.'

'Making you happy makes me happy. How was your day?'

'One more. Or one less. Depending on your viewpoint.'

'After I left yesterday, I wondered why you don't look for work in Guadeloupe. I'm sure there's no lack of hotels over there. And what with your experience ...'

'I've thought about it. I know I could find something. It's just that I was there on holiday. And I always want to be on holiday.'

'You'd only get bored.'

'I don't think so. Some people always need to be doing something. Not me. I just want to be.'

'Like pandas.'

'Sorry?'

'I said pandas, but I might as well have said lizards, or anything.'

'Exactly. I know I'm not that intelligent. You've seen, the few books I own are just there to fill the space. It doesn't bother me. I could spend whole days lying on a beach in the sun and not thinking of anything, not even dreaming or making the effort to live. I'm a big lazy so and so.'

When she laughed, you wanted to climb inside her mouth and never get out.

'How is your Peking duck?'

'A bit dry, but it's okay.'

The usual cup of rice wine, on the house, with a pair

of buttocks painted on the bottom, rounded the dinner off. No other customers had come in. It was like being at home, just the two of them. They could have grabbed each other, there and then, on the dirty tablecloth covered in soy and chilli sauce stains and gone at it. The staff wouldn't have minded. Madeleine would certainly have been keen. There, on the table. Without thinking. Without dreaming. Without making the effort to live …

'Would you like me to walk you home?'

The rain had stopped, exhausted. The sky was completely drained. A few streetlights stood sleeping like blind sentries.

'Here we are then. See you tomorrow, Madeleine.'

'You're a tease!' she said as her mouth crushed Gabriel's.

Building C, stairwell 3, the rubbish storeroom. It was there, in the creeping darkness, that big Babeth introduced generations of kids to their first French kiss. Her tongue plunged into Gabriel's mouth with demonic force. It wrapped around his tongue like the boa constrictor that had captured Tarzan in the comic he had read the day before. It wasn't a tongue but an enormous muscle, a tensed, turning bicep which filled his mouth, burrowing ever deeper and suffocating him. The only way out was to bite down on the piece of wriggling meat. Babeth howled out in pain, throwing punches and pulling his hair. He let go and ran off through the dark labyrinthine cellars, the taste of blood in his mouth, the beast screaming insults and spitting curses from deep within her lair. Two of his friends were waiting their turn at the top of the stairs.

'Well, how was … Fuck! You're covered in blood!'

The three of them ran off as fast as their legs could carry them. Gabriel was twelve.

'I'm sorry, Madeleine. I'd rather not.'

'Am I so disgusting?'

In the glow of a streetlight Madeleine's face began to dissolve in a whirlpool of doubt. Gabriel hugged her and patted her gently on the shoulder. He had done the same for José after the experience with the red lorry.

'Not at all, Madeleine. I promise you. You're very desirable. It's just that I'd rather not.'

Like José, she was sobbing. Then, suddenly pulling away from him, she spat out the word 'Arsehole' before slamming the door in his face.

Gabriel thought that when the world ended it wouldn't make a sound. A little moan, at most.

'"You're not leaving the table until you finish your food!" I didn't like soup so what did he expect? I didn't care – I had all the time in the world. I would've waited there until my plate was full of maggots. An hour later, he chucked me out. I was left out on the doorstep with my plate on my knees, all because he needed the table for his stupid jigsaw puzzles. The local cats all knew the routine. In five minutes my plate was empty and I was allowed back in. In, out, in, out ... That's what I've done all my life, always between two doors. But now he's gone for good I don't know what side I'm on. You know, Gabriel, it's a strange feeling. It's as if I've nowhere to go, as if I have to get out myself. Rita! You're making a pig of yourself. This isn't some dump, you know.'

It was the most expensive restaurant in town. Two stars and on the cusp of a third. Opulent. Someone had knocked on Gabriel's door that morning. It was the saxophone guy,

Marc, with a smile that stretched from ear to ear.

'That's it! He's dead, stone-cold dead! We've won the lottery! Rita and I want to take you out for a meal, to pay you back for the peanuts.'

His father had passed away during the night. He had fallen out of bed – a bit surprising according to the nurse, who said the old man hadn't been able to move in ages. But considering the amount of medicine they shovelled into old people these days, anything was possible. The solicitor had called Marc at 8 a.m.

'And that's not all! With the house and garden in the middle of town alone I've got enough to last me two, maybe three, lifetimes. But the old bastard had investments all over the place too! I'm seeing the solicitor about everything later. Rita, don't you think two plates of snails as a starter are enough?'

Gabriel had only eaten one portion. The food was excellent, especially the chopped morels. His breath heavy with alcohol, Marc whispered in Gabriel's ear, 'I'm doing a runner tonight. I can't have her cramping my new lifestyle.'

Rita smiled at him as she wiped her plate clean with a large hunk of bread. She certainly hadn't heard Marc, but she was no fool and she didn't care. They loved each other, or, rather, the complicity that had united them had over time come to resemble love. They could kill each other and not hold it against each other. That's life though, isn't it? As a result of travelling in the same carriage stinking of feet, you manage to find your little corner of intimacy; you understand each other. You get used to each other's smells and tricky ways; you take on the habits of the other. Familiarity is everything, no need to think or choose; you feel as at ease with the other person as you do with yourself. The tatty old slippers, the bed hair, the hair left in the comb, scenes from life which surprise us each morning. Yes, it isn't always a pretty sight looking in the mirror. It's true that there are days when you just want to smash it, but you don't because, if you did, you'd be left staring at the wall, and the wall is even uglier than you are.

'How are your sweetbreads?' asked Marc.

'Delicious!'

'I can't stand offal. It smells too much of insides and the thing with insides—'

'Insides?'

'You don't know what's in them. So when are you leaving?'

'I don't know. It depends which way the wind's blowing.'

Marc frowned, taken aback, trying to fathom the hidden meaning in Gabriel's ambiguous response. Unable to find it, he shrugged his shoulders, emptied his glass and held the bottle up to the maître d'.

'Another,' he shouted.

Rita was playing with her napkin, having polished off her stuffed quail.

'I used to be able to fold all sort of things, like fans or cones. It's weird – I can't do it any more. I think it's the wrong kind of material.'

'Come off it!' Marc laughed. 'The material? Why don't you go and wash your hands and mouth. It looks like a dog's arse.'

Rita didn't know whether to laugh or cry as she looked at Marc with her cowlike eyes. She picked up the napkin, folding it into a small triangle, and held it under her nose, humming 'How Much is that Doggie in the Window'. She stood up, knocking over her chair, which a waiter rushed to pick up.

'You're right, Marco. I need to go and powder my nose.'

Rita zigzagged unsteadily between the tables towards the door that led to the toilets. Marc pulled two huge cigars out of his pocket and offered one to Gabriel, who declined. He bit the end off one and spat it onto his plate. He didn't know how to blow smoke rings, only shapeless clouds.

'What are you going to do now that you're rich?' asked Gabriel.

'Lounge about like a rich person! I've lived enough as a poor person. It won't make much of a difference, except that I'll be able to eat when I'm hungry and be warm when it's cold. You have to make use of what you've got, don't you?'

'Absolutely.'

'The only thing I'll miss, to start with, will be Rita.'

'So why leave her?'

'That's the way it is. The poor with the poor, the rich with the rich. Otherwise, what would happen? Everyone has to stick to their own kind as my dad used to say. It's not my fault if I'm now rich! This cigar is disgusting. It must be as old as Methuselah; it's as ancient and dry as his heart. You know what he used to do?'

'No, what?'

'He used to get a hard-on when they bathed him. A

hard-on! The old bastard! Standing to attention! No joke. Crazy, eh ...!'

Rita was coming towards them, her face plastered with make-up. She looked like something out of a Greek tragedy. She was trembling from head to toe.

'Marco, I don't feel very well. I want to go back to the hotel.'

It was Marc's turn to go white. He got up, leaving a handful of notes on the table, and took Rita by the shoulder.

'Stupid bitch. Not here, shit, not here. Hold it together. Sorry about this, Gabriel. We'll see you later.'

On the walls of the church, the saints sagged. They looked unwell – haggard, gaunt, unshaven with greasy hair, overburdened, their eyes heavy with mystical worry. Even the haloes which glowed above their heads failed to brighten them up. They were exhausted. Evidently, the Last Supper menu hadn't been that appealing. That was why, no doubt, they were all eyeing up the baby Jesus resting in the arms of the Virgin Mary like a suckling pig, plump and sweetie pink. 'This is my body …' You shouldn't tempt the devil that lurks at the bottom of your stomach. The smell of incense that permeated these places was reminiscent of the smell of meat that clings to bad Greek restaurants. With a little more effort, the pale light glinting through the stained glass could have brought a psychedelic touch to the emptiness, but it was happy to go where directed. It shone like a little celestial pee-pee. After Marc and Rita had left the restaurant in a hurry, Gabriel had gone off in search of somewhere to digest his food in peace. He had thought about going to the cinema and taking a seat in the dark, but the problem with the cinema was that the films were usually quite loud, with stories which were more annoying than real life. The church seemed like a better idea. The straw-seated chairs were perhaps a little less comfortable than those in a cinema but entry was free and he wouldn't have to put up with any popcorn eaters.

He must have nodded off for a bit because when he opened his eyes again he became aware of an elderly woman sitting next to him grinding her badly fitting dentures between her thin lips. The impression was of an elderly bird that had fallen out of a nest, its beak flattened by an unsuccessful landing. An impression heightened by thinning blue-rinsed hair rising in a quiff above a wrinkled forehead, a protruding chin, prominent cheekbones and a neck with folds of soft skin over an unswallowable Adam's apple.

'You were snoring,' the old woman said.

'Forgive me.'

'That's not up to me. It's up to the Lord God Almighty,' she said. 'You know what?'

'What?'

'My dog was poisoned this morning.'

'Your dog?'

'That's what I said.'

'I'm sorry.'

'I've just lodged a complaint at the police station because I know who did it!'

'That's the right thing to do.'

'Between you and me, I didn't really like the dog. I only went to the police on principle.'

'I see.'

'He was horrible. He barked all the time and was bad-tempered as well! He belonged to my former husband, a real mongrel.'

The old woman hadn't yet turned to look at Gabriel. She kept her gaze fixed straight ahead on the altar, munching on her false teeth, gripping the handbag that sat on her bony knees.

'It was a black and white mongrel called Georges. They used to go hunting and fishing together.'

'Your dog was called Georges?'

'Yes, like my husband. It was his idea. "That way, if I get lost," he said, "all I have to do is call out my own name!" It used to make him laugh. He died a nasty death.'

'Your husband?'

'No, the dog. It wasn't a pretty sight, believe me. It was terrible. My husband's death was much quicker. He decapitated himself with his chainsaw when he was out pruning the cherry trees. He didn't suffer. Well, that's what the doctor said. But what does he know? He's never been decapitated!'

'And your dog?'

'Poisoned meat. Rat poison. You know, those little red pellets. His vomit was full of them.'

'That's terrible.'

'Yes, terrible. His eyes bulged and his tongue was hanging out as if trying to escape his mouth. Animals are stupid, especially dogs. Perhaps it's the effect of the people they spend time with. They only think of themselves. They're not like us, they don't have a soul.'

With a crooked finger, she made the sign of the cross so rapidly it looked like an aeroplane propeller.

'Are you waiting for Father Mauro?'

'No.'

'He's always late. He's a drinker.'

'Ah.'

'Yes, he's a drinker. And he masturbates in front of St Rita as well. I've seen him do it. Everyone has their flaws, I suppose.'

'That's true.'

'I've only come for confession. I've got an appointment at the hairdresser's at four o'clock and it's already twenty to. I won't be long. I've just got to tell him that I was the one who killed Georges but that I've blamed it on my neighbour. Speak of the devil, here he is now ... Have a nice day.'

'And you.'

The old lady got up and scurried shakily down the aisle to meet a jovial-looking priest of the sort you'd find on a cheese packet. God had no need to worry, business was good.

The street swarmed with extras but there was no audience, or director. And there was probably no script either. Everybody wandered around without aim or purpose, hesitant and unable to find their place. Perhaps that was the intention. It wasn't unusual to bump into the same person in different parts of the town; grim-faced, lost in thought and waiting, in the absence of a revelation, for some sort of sign. The entire town seemed on standby. The sky was equally unsettled, with threatening clouds, light rain and intermittent flashes of lightning. Swarms of minuscule gnats, impervious to swiping hands, buzzed overhead. Nothing made sense. If being alive was just a hobby then how could you be sure that there would be a tomorrow? Just as there was no guarantee there had been a yesterday. It was a day to kill someone for no reason.

Gabriel had bought himself a frying pan, a pot and a camping stove. He was going to eat alone in his hotel room tonight. Ham, mashed potato and chestnut purée. He'd had enough of them. He didn't want to see them or listen to their whining. And yet, without realising, he found himself in front of the Faro. The bar was crowded, like a teeming fish tank. Noticing him outside, José waved his cloth in Gabriel's direction, inviting him inside. Now the panda and José looked so alike it was hard to distinguish them; they both grinned like Cheshire cats. As Gabriel didn't move José dashed out from behind the counter and opened the door wide.

'What on earth are you doing? Come on in!'

'It's fine, I—'

'She's opened her eyes, Gabriel! She spoke to me!'

'What did she say?'

'Joke.'

'Joke?'

'Joke, or poke, or folk, I didn't really understand. She wasn't quite with it but she said it three times, with her eyes wide open! The doctors were completely baffled. Come on in! You know, Gabriel, you and me. Now it's going to be ...'

José crossed his fingers; his eyes welled up with tears. He slapped Gabriel on the shoulder and pushed him inside. Where had this spontaneous generation of carefree youth who laughed, sang, told jokes and emptied glass after glass come from? All it took was a little watering for them to pop up like mushrooms from between the slats in the floorboards. What use is a miracle if there is no one there to witness it?

'No, not beer. It's champagne time!' José exclaimed.

'By the way, I tried to call you at your hotel to tell you the good news but you weren't there. The girl on reception said she'd let you know. I thought I'd invite her along. I hope you don't mind?'

'No, not at all. Here's to the end of your worries, José. I'm very happy for you.'

'You'll see. You're going to get on really well with Marie. Everything will be like before, but even better.'

'I'm sure it will.'

The searing rays of sunlight which set the terrace ablaze werediffused as they struck the motionless beaded curtain, so that all that passed into the living room was speckles of light, instantly swallowed up in blue shadow. Blandine was asleep on the couch, her mouth slightly open, her brow misted with the perspiration of sleep. One arm was folded under her head and the other hung by her side, her fingers brushing the coir mat. The cats lay at her feet, breathing in sync. Somewhere in the distance, a long way away, someone played a piano. The same passage of music, over and over. A newborn baby cried, a boat came into port, a fly landed on the ceiling. The house creaked, whispering gossip. The smell of the barbecue, dried herbs, charcoal and melon skin lingered in the air. On the first floor, in a hammock that Gabriel had fitted the day before, Juliette rocked back and forth while sucking her thumb and dreaming of unexplored futures. Gabriel closed his book. Every page seemed like a closed shutter. Focusing on anything else but the sweetness of this magical moment seemed inappropriate, even rude. Yet despite his best efforts he wasn't able to let go, to surrender to sleep, to experience the same feeling as the others:

his wife, his daughter, the cats, the fly. He felt excluded from everybody's bliss, from all the innocence. But he didn't know why. It was as if he had committed a crime of which he had no memory. A surge of injustice mixed with guilty despair rose within him and threatened to suffocate him. He bit into his closed fist to stop himself from screaming out as tears rolled down his cheeks. He should never have taken the plane the day after.

'Gabriel?'

Madeleine's face appeared through a fog of cigarette smoke. She had changed her hair, which was now held back on either side with combs. It suited her, made her look younger. Just behind her stood Rita, her badly lipsticked lips stretched in a crooked, timid smile.

'You look like you've seen a ghost. Shall we get a table? The bar's too busy.'

Rita instinctively headed over to the same table that she had shared with Marc two days earlier. Force of habit. The three of them sat down and José served each of them a glass of champagne.

'It's on the house! And there's more where that came from. Gabriel's like a brother to me. Just tell him whatever you want and I'll be right over.'

The women sat side by side, the curly little hairs on the back of their necks visible in the mirror behind them. Madeleine raised her glass.

'I'm not sure what we're celebrating, but cheers!'

They clinked glasses. People are fragile. Hard and fragile, like glass.

'For someone who doesn't know anyone round here …'

'It's all down to chance. José was the first person I met. Well, apart from you. Do you remember, when I first arrived, I asked you if you could recommend a restaurant?'

'And Rita? You know each other, don't you?'

'That's by chance as well.'

'So that's how you live, by chance?'

'That's right, yes, just like everybody else. And what about you, Rita? What brings you here, if you don't mind me asking?'

'Me? My chance is called Marco!'

She smiled bitterly and downed her drink in one. Some people wore their misfortune with elegance. Rita was one of them. Her heart, hammered by a thousand blows, echoed like a gong, a bronze shield on which fate could make no dent.

'He's buggered off. I was stuffed when I got back to the hotel after lunch. I collapsed and when I woke up he'd vanished.'

'He'll be back, I'm sure. Didn't he have a meeting with his solicitor?'

'You don't take your toothbrush to the solicitor. Gone, with his suitcase, without leaving me a penny and without settling the room, the bastard. Can I get another?'

'Of course. José, do you mind?'

'Thanks. Excuse me while I nip to the loo.'

José refilled the glasses and whispered in Gabriel's ear, loud enough for Madeleine to hear.

'So then, you rascal. You don't hang around, do you? Two at a time!'

Madeleine covered her mouth to stifle a laugh, then said seriously, 'Poor soul. I think she's hooked on drugs. Have you seen her pupils? They're pinpricks! When she came down from her room earlier she was in a right state, her eyes smeared with make-up. She looked a total wreck. I saw this Marco leave, but as she was upstairs I didn't think anything of it. What a bastard! I'd just got off the phone to your friend José. I felt sorry for her and she told me you knew each other so I suggested she come along. Is that all right?'

'Yes, of course it's all right, Madeleine.'

'Where did you meet them?'

'Here. I gave them some peanuts.'

'Peanuts?'

'Yes. They had a saxophone for sale. I bought it to give to José's kids.'

'A saxophone? You do some strange things!'

'Do I?'

'Yes. You've only been here four or five days and already you know so many people. It's amazing how you've become part of their lives. You make yourself at home wherever you go, don't you?'

'I don't mean to. I swear it's not my fault. Do you think it's wrong?'

'I didn't say it was wrong! You just make my head spin a bit. You're nowhere and everywhere at the same time. I don't know what to do with this poor girl. And I don't know what I'm going to say to my boss – he's not the sympathetic type.'

'I'll pay her bill, don't worry.'

'That's kind of you. What's going to happen to her though?'

'I don't know.'

'You don't think she'd commit suicide, do you?'

'No, she's not that type. She wants more from life.'

'Here she is now.'

The men standing at the bar turned and nudged each other as Rita walked past. She wasn't beautiful, but she had something about her and knew how to flaunt it. She crossed the room nonchalantly, rolling her hips, revelling in the lusty stares of the men.

'Men! Well, you have to have them. Lots of them though, not one! I've finished with that!'

She knew how to laugh. It was a hearty laugh, intelligent and frank. She didn't hold back. Madeleine looked on admiringly, with a touch of envy.

'I feel good with you two. If I had the cash, I'd take you both out for something to eat. I'm starving!'

Rita had an urge for red meat and chips. The only thing now remaining on her plate was the bone from her steak and a smear of mustard. She had been to the toilet twice and had downed three bottles of beer. She was like a time bomb; you never knew exactly when it might go off. Madeleine had taken them to a Western-themed restaurant. It suited the situation perfectly. Beefy blokes came here to eat beef and drink beer, which clouded their gaze with a mixture of guilt and greed.

'Have you ever seen a white poppy?' Rita asked.

'No.'

'I found one once. I was young, about eight years old.

It was a Sunday in spring. I used to live in a little village called Subligny, near Sens. I was at a picnic with my cousins, uncles and aunts. We made posies of wild flowers: daisies and cornflowers. The weather was gorgeous. It had been a long, long winter. The grass came up to my chin. The sky was a picture-postcard blue. We laughed and chased each other while the men opened bottles and the women laid out the tablecloths, pâté, ham and salad. It was a wonderful day. And then I found it, there on its own, a white poppy. White! I fell down in front of it as though it were the Virgin Mary. It swayed in the wind, which swept through the field. There were others next to it, normal red ones that didn't care about being picked or trodden on, just normal poppies, you know. I plucked it at its base and ran with it, holding it up in the air like a flag, to show my family. They were all amazed at my albino poppy. They took my photo. I was as pleased as punch. Here, look, I've got the photo.'

Rita rummaged around in her miniature handbag, the bag that contained her whole life, and pulled out a shiny purse from which she picked out a yellowing photograph with curled corners and scalloped edges like a *petit beurre* biscuit. It showed a laughing, chubby little girl, with a Joan of Arc haircut, brandishing a skinny flower in both hands above her head. Behind her, against the backdrop of a milky sky, stood the blurred image of a small scowling boy. Rita, the queen of an unforgettable day.

'You can tell it's me, can't you? I pressed it between two paper plates so I wouldn't forget it. But after, because everybody was drunk, it got lost, probably thrown in the bin or something. It wasn't a big deal. Whether they're red or white, poppies don't last.'

The photo passed from Gabriel to Madeleine.

'It's funny, I've got similar photos of me when I was a kid, this age with the same haircut and the same outfit. I used to wear these awful glasses. God, I was so ugly! You don't look so bad, Rita. So what are you going to do now?'

'I don't know. I can't decide. I've always been like that. I don't like deciding things. My only options are nothing or anything. What would you choose? I've spent my life following different people to different places. That's why Marco was good for me. He always knew where he was going. As often as not it was straight into a wall but at least it was something, right? Why did that bastard have to leave me? I'd better not go anywhere. I don't know much, but I've got this gut feeling. He's going to need me – I'd stake my life on it. You're a man, Gabriel. What do you think?'

'I don't know. Yes, maybe wait a while.'

'Yes, I'll do that. The only problem is I'm completely broke.'

'I'll take care of that. I'll settle your room.'

'That's very kind. We could share the same room if you want. That would save money.'

'I'm not sure that's such a good idea.'

'Ah, okay. Oh, I'm sorry, Madeleine. You know what it's like when you get wrapped up in your own problems; you don't think about anybody else. I'm stupid.'

The two women turned to one another and looked into each other's eyes as if staring into a mirror. Madeleine took Rita's hand.

'There's nothing going on between me and Gabriel. Isn't that right, Gabriel?'

Gabriel didn't answer. He stared at his hands, which were flat on the table, as though dealt out in a card game. He was thinking about the ham and mashed potato he had planned for himself that evening.

Madeleine pulled herself up like a ship's figurehead, her sumptuous chest thrust forth against the wind and tide, heading for distant lands. 'You can stay at mine for a bit, Rita. We'll work something out.'

'Why would you do that for me? We hardly know each other.'

'I don't know. Ask Gabriel. He must know. He knows everything.'

Love me tender, love me sweet, never let me go. The music at the end of the film. The restaurant's lights went out one by one. The bill paid, it was time to digest the steak and chips, to sleep off the beer wherever they could. Tomorrow was another day.

They soon forgot about the rain. It coursed from the rooftops and down the gutters as naturally as blood through veins. Madeleine's umbrella was too small for the three of them so, depending on the size of the pavement, Gabriel walked behind, in front or to the side.

'Well then, goodnight.'

The two women stood glued to the umbrella handle, watching Gabriel dripping under the streetlight.

'You can't just leave us like that! Come upstairs for a drink. You've got something to drink, haven't you, Madeleine?'

'Yes, but he doesn't want to.'

'Another time. I have to get up early tomorrow. Goodnight.'

The women watched him turn and walk away, hopping over puddles, hunched over like a question mark.

'He's one of a kind that one. Do you have a crush on him?' asked Rita.

'Maybe,' said Madeleine.

'He reminds me of a priest sometimes. But he is a man after all and you never know with men. What about women, Madeleine? Do you like women?'

The sound of their laughter matched the rippling noise of the rain on their umbrella. They looked like a two-headed bat. The town yawned, the rooftops overflowed.

The only thing left in the freezer compartment was a huge calf's tongue studded with ice crystals. It was otherwise empty, just like the apartment. Gabriel had spent the day waiting for it to defrost on the chopping board. A whole day watching the mute tongue's slow thaw. He didn't have anything else to do. At about seven o'clock he threw the tongue into a pot of simmering stock and made a punchy sauce with tomatoes, gherkins and shallots. There was enough to feed an army. He ate it all though, the tongue that said nothing, out on the terrace, until it made him sick. All that remained were fragments of bone and cartilage. The telephone had rung as he vomited, his head over the toilet bowl, his hands gripping the porcelain sides. It didn't matter. He didn't have anything to say to anybody. Wrapped in the cats' tartan rug, he made his way back out onto the terrace. It was warm but he shivered as he looked up at the sickle moon scything the stars. Usually, at this time, Juliette would have been asleep, sucking her thumb,

and Blandine would have been drawing at her work bench
with the cats running around. But he had just vomited a whole
calf's tongue and had run out of words to describe the night
and the sea and what he was still doing alive.

'What are you thinking about?'

'A calf's tongue.'

'You're unbelievable. All you think about is food. So how did it go with the girls last night?'

'Good. We went out for a meal and then I went home.'

'Alone?'

'Alone.'

'I don't get you. They were all over you, especially the tall one, the one from the hotel. What's her name again?'

'Madeleine.'

'Man, all you need to do is click your fingers. She's a good-looking girl. And the other one isn't bad either. She's a different type. So you didn't do either of them?'

'They're friends, just friends.'

'Well, it's your business. But it's a waste, all the same. Anyway, what do you think of my flowers?'

'Very nice.'

'They're orchids. They come from some island or something. Have a look in the back again to see if they're still okay, will you? I bought them early this morning.'

Gabriel leant over the back seat. Orchids were ugly. They looked like photos of venereal diseases in medical books.

'They look fine.'

'Good. Look at that idiot in front. Overtaking again

and again. Look, there he is, stopped at the traffic lights. It serves him right! After the hospital I'm going to call the children to tell them to be very good when their mother comes back. She's been through a lot and it'll take her time to get back on her feet. Or we could go and see them, if you've got nothing else to do, of course.

'If you want.'

'Here we are then. I think I'm going to take my tie off; I'm going to explode.'

It was white as far as the eye could see. The waiting room was as sterile as an iceberg. Hidden behind the enormous bouquet of flowers, José looked like a small, solitary tree.

'Right, so I'll see you here later then?'

'Yup, I'll be here. Off you go.'

Gabriel sat down on a plastic chair and leafed through magazines filled with smiling movie stars, politicians and television personalities. They were all tanned with white teeth and blue eyes. They weren't allowed to be unhappy. They had been hoisted onto a pedestal, doomed to never-ending happiness. By contrast, for the ordinary mortal, unhappiness was almost a duty. Drips, Zimmer frames, wheelchairs, he could have any misfortune he wanted. Dragging himself around, shuffling in his slippers, wrapped in an oversized dressing gown, smoking a cigarette, drinking weak cups of coffee, waiting for family or ogling those of others, an ashen complexion, a vacant eye, hollow cheeks, always waiting. Waiting and living off simple platitudes like 'good luck', 'keep strong' and 'see you later'. Obviously little people could only have little thoughts. They apologised for everything they did. 'Sorry, do you mind if I take a look at that magazine?', 'Excuse me, which floor are you going to?', 'Excuse me, do you have the time?', 'I'm sorry for still being here, all repulsive and ill.' Nurses laughed as they pushed trolleys stacked with lunch trays, wafting the smells of hospital food, lukewarm and flavourless. Their shoes clicked on the floor tiles. Remembering a Brassens tune about a horse dutifully pulling its cart through rain and mud, Gabriel hummed, '*C'était un petit cheval blanc, tous derrière, tous derrière* ...'

The doors of lift B opened. José walked out. He looked like a rain-drenched panda. He passed Gabriel without registering him.

'José? José?'

José turned round. His face was empty of emotion, a mirror with nobody standing in front of it.

'Are you okay?'

'She's not dead, but she's never going to wake up. She's sleeping. That's it, she's sleeping. I'm tired, Gabriel. I want to go home. I want to go to sleep as well.'

The croissant didn't taste very nice. He had only wanted one after being lured in by the artificial baking scent pumped out by the shop. The smell had reminded him of his childhood. He hadn't really needed either a croissant or memories of his childhood. His sense of smell had fooled him. He sat on a bench and made crumbs, which he threw to the pigeons. One by one they came and belligerently tapped their beaks like mechanical tools. It wasn't a beautiful sight, but it grew on him.

'You shouldn't feed the bastards.'

The voice came from a man sitting at the other end of the bench. He looked curiously like a pigeon himself. Slightly fat, with googly eyes and a pointed nose, he was wrapped in a grey waterproof.

'Why not?'

'They shit on my window. They shit on my car. They shit on the church statues. They shit everywhere. As if there isn't enough shit in the world!'

'They're birds.'

'Exactly! They've got all the fields and woods to do it in. But no, they come and shit on us, thanks to people like you who feed them. And, besides, they aren't birds. They're rats. Flying rats. The souls of dead rats taking revenge on sewer workers. To them, we're all sewer workers. In a way, they're right, but we still have to watch out! Look at them scratching themselves. They're full of disease. Completely inedible.'

'Have you tried them?'

'Of course. I trapped them with birdlime. They're much tougher than crows. Crows are useful though. They're cleaners; they only feed on dead things. Imagine a battlefield without crows. It'd be a real rubbish dump! Apart from carrying a message from one trench to the other, what has a pigeon ever done on a battlefield? And what do we use them for now? We've got other communication methods now … and, well, that's a topic for another day. Because they used to hang out with soldiers, because they think they're heroes, saviours of France, pigeons have got too big for their boots. They're so full of themselves. And that's why they shit on us. Humanity will end up swimming in the shit of diseased pigeons. They're all diseased. They come and go and pick up every germ there is. It's awful. It's like a modern-day Pompeii!'

'But what can we do about it?'

'Kill as many as we can and send the others back home.'

'Back home?'

'They come from somewhere, don't they? St Mark's

Square in Venice, for example. We could kill two birds with one stone. They'd infect all the Japanese, American, Swedish and Bulgarian tourists. There's bound to be a pigeon loft there somewhere. Either way, if we don't give them anything to eat, then they'll go away. And, anyway, you're feeding them junk. Where did you buy your croissant?'

'The snack bar on the main road.'

'I knew it! Can you imagine what kind of shit they'll be dropping on us now?'

'You're right. I hadn't thought.'

The man shrugged his shoulders and scratched his head vigorously. Dandruff fell from his greasy hair and quickly covered his collar. He got rid of it by flapping his jacket, his elbows bent, as he stretched out his neck and cleared his throat.

'Seagulls aren't much better, you know. I once spent a night in a hotel in Cancale. My room overlooked the restaurant's rubbish bins. I didn't sleep a wink. And swallows? You think they herald the spring? Spring doesn't exist any more! I hate birds, all birds. The skies are too full. It's our rubbish bins which attract them, our monstrous rubbish bins. I leave nothing for them, young man. I finish everything. I don't leave them a crumb! I'm even going to leave my body to science. There'll be nothing left of François Dacis, nothing! As if I hadn't existed. And of that I'm proud!'

'That's all very admirable.'

'You don't need to tell me. Here, between you and me, I don't even trust angels.'

'Angels?'

'Yes, angels. They fly around with all the dirty birds and so they're infected as well! Bird flu and the rest, I tell you! Angels used to have nice plump faces like well-fed toddlers blowing on their trumpets. But today, young man, they all look like junkies. They just hover around not giving a fuck about anything.'

He scratched his head furiously again, shaking the dandruff off while clearing his throat with a cooing sound. There was a feverish look in his eye.

'The apocalypse will come from above. Like at Hiroshima. Since the big boss copped it, anarchy has ruled the clouds. It's time to go underground, young man, I'm telling you!'

The old man pulled a crumpled piece of paper from his pocket and smoothed it out on his knees with his forearm. It was some kind of blueprint.

'Bomb shelter, fallout shelter. Anti-pigeon, anti-everything. Ten metres square with four-metre-thick reinforced Swedish reinforced-concrete walls, buried fifty metres below good old Breton soil. I've thought of everything. The heating is provided by the toilet waste and the water is triple filtered. The living room is there, with a sofa, TV, radio and bar. All mod cons. Here is where the stockpiles are kept, next to the kitchen: wheat, rice, corn, pasta and tinned food. And the armoury. You never know! And the medicine area: aspirin, antiseptic, dressings. And the best bit, a cellar! Ten metres further down with everything you'd ever need. It could last me sixty years, maybe more! I'll die there, but at least it'll be of natural causes. What do you think? Great, eh?'

'Magnificent. Where is it?'

The man narrowed his eyes and tapped the side of his head.

'Top secret, my friend. It's all up here.'

He rolled up his sleeve and stared at his watchless wrist.

'Good God, I'd better go. How about ten euros?'

'Ten euros? For what?'

'My survival plan. You can have it for ten euros. Five for something to eat and then five for a wash.'

'Okay then.'

'You've got yourself a good deal there. But no more feeding the pigeons. You promise?'

'Yes, I promise.'

'Well, good evening, young man. It's getting dark; the weather's turning. You'd better go home. It's been a pleasure.'

The old man got up. He rolled his shoulders, puffed out his chest and stuck his nose in the air. He opened his waterproof and strode determinedly off, scattering the pigeons as he went.

On another bench, two teenagers sat not kissing. The boy was looking down at his enormous new trainers, size 12 perhaps. The young girl was twisting a strand of hair between her fingers and holding it up to her lips as a moustache. They both looked extremely bored. It suited them. The sky was the colour of frogspawn absorbing joy and sorrow with the same indifference. Gabriel rubbed his hands together. He had washed them ten times that day but still they smelt of the hospital. José had insisted on sleeping in one of his children's beds. The three sleeping tablets he had taken would do him until tomorrow, his big boar head resting on a Mickey Mouse pillowcase.

Rita and I waited for you until eight o'clock. Come and join us at my place if you want – Madeleine.

The note had been slipped under the door. Gabriel didn't know whether or not to go. The ravioli simmered on the camping stove in front of the open window. A church bell struck nine as if testing the density of the air. He hadn't eaten ravioli out of a tin since he was a child. He used to eat them all the time. He used to love them. Now though, even when they were covered in Parmesan, he found them disgusting, like eating spoonfuls of vomit. Yet, perhaps out of respect for his childhood, he finished them all. Afterwards, he cleaned the pan in the washbasin. The water, reddened by the tomato sauce, slowly swirled down the plughole with a revolting gurgle. He looked at himself in the mirror and saw he had sauce around his mouth. Like blood, it was difficult to get rid of tomato sauce completely. There was always some left behind.

Months after … the accident he kept finding tiny flecks on the sole of a shoe or on a button. He ended up seeing them everywhere, like strewn confetti after a carnival. He closed his eyes for a moment. The darkness enveloped him. Only the searing glow of the strip light on which he was resting his forehead remained. He left the bathroom in a hurry, threw on his jacket and slammed the door behind him. He raced down the stairs and flung himself into the street. On the pavement, he lifted his nose to the sky, took a deep breath and filled his lungs with as much of the manure-rich night air as he could. Slowly the scorching of the fluorescent tube faded away, much like a white-hot knife plunged into a tub of cold water. He strode determinedly off like an old steam engine. He reached out his hand and touched everything he passed: the freezing metal pole of a one-way sign, the corners of a tattered poster, a rough brick wall. He had to feel everything around him, dry, wet, hot and cold, to convince himself it was real. He wasn't sure of anything. He moved faster as if trying to escape from a predator – his shadow perhaps? Or the past, which was swiftly catching up with him? He could feel its icy breath on his neck. Around him the town was falling apart like a boat in a storm. The tar was rising up, the sky falling down. He was a panting wreck by the time he reached Madeleine's flat.

'Ah, Gabriel! We were wondering if you were coming. What's wrong? You look like you've seen a ghost!'

'No, I'm fine. I was running because of the rain.'

'But it isn't raining.'

'Exactly. I wanted to get here before it started raining.'

The door closed behind him, leaving the monster on the other side. Indoors, there was only the comfort of the here and now. Rita was sprawled on the couch wearing a tracksuit and slippers which slopped off her feet, probably borrowed from Madeleine. It hadn't taken her long to become part of the furniture.

'Look who it is! We didn't think you'd come.'

Rita sat up and patted the cushion next to her in invitation. Gabriel sat down and caught his breath. The room was soft, warm and sweet. Madeleine sat opposite the sofa on a pouffe. As she poured Gabriel a glass of cognac, her dressing gown hung forward to reveal the curve of her breast. She must have just come out of the bathroom. Her hair was wet and she smelt of soap, dewy and clean. Gabriel finished his glass in one. Slowly, his whole body began to relax. He should have come sooner. The two women glanced at each other. Rita poured herself a large drink.

'We thought you might make us a bit of supper.'

'Haven't you eaten?'

'Yes, of course, don't worry. We had a little tea party. Is everything okay? Do you want another drink?'

'Yes, please.'

Madeleine put her hand on Gabriel's knee.

'Is it José's wife?'

'No. Well, yes. Maybe. She's fallen into another coma. No one's sure when she'll wake up. Perhaps never. It could last weeks or months. Even years.'

'And what about José?'

'I took him back to his place. He's asleep now. I gave

him some sleeping tablets. We'll see how he is tomorrow.'

Rita stood up, emptied her glass and put on a CD. It was a tango dance track, the kind radio stations usually played. She sat back down, practically in Gabriel's lap.

'I could never stand "Sleeping Beauty" stories.'

'Rita!'

'What? It's true. Even when I was little I never liked stupid fairy tales. They were either so scary I couldn't understand how adults could read them to kids or they were unbelievably soppy and annoying. It's no surprise that the world is as daft as it is if we're telling stories like that to our kids.'

'I loved "The Little Mermaid".'

'Jesus, that's another one. A bimbo who goes to the trouble of getting legs that hurt like hell for a guy who ends up dumping her for somebody else. That's morally okay, is it? You've got to be twisted to write something like that. And, anyway, it's always the women who pay the price in the end in those stories. "The Little Match Girl"? Dies of cold. "Little Thumbling"? Who ends up being eaten? The ogre's daughters, of course. Aren't I right, Gabriel? You know everything.'

'I saw the Little Mermaid in Copenhagen.'

'And what was she like?'

'Small.'

'Of course she was! They didn't haggle over the size of the statues for Stalin, de Gaulle or Émile Zola, did they? But for the Little Mermaid! Women are on the bottom rung of society; we're like a school of sardines surrounded by sharks.'

Madeleine smiled. The sea was at low tide. She looked like she didn't care about the status of women. She was daydreaming, floating in the sea somewhere off the coast of Guadeloupe.

'You should never leave the water,' Madeleine said. 'Men or women. Everything is weightless in the water. We glide and brush up against each other, bob up and down. There's no noise. Everything is quiet, the mind clear.'

She must have been a bit drunk. She stood up and spun round on her toes, her eyes closed, her body in thrall to the music, her dressing gown flaring out.

'There was nothing before, there'll be nothing after and we don't give a damn about what goes on in between. Why? Why?'

Rita reached over to the lamp beside the couch and turned it off, plunging the room into darkness. The only light came from the streetlamp. The room resembled a fish tank. Rita sidled up to Gabriel.

'She's beautiful, isn't she?'

'Yes, she is. Very.'

'Do you fancy her?'

He had bought a fish tank for Juliette on her fourth birthday, but she hadn't wanted to put fish in it. She just liked the plastic algae and the little toy diver that knelt in front of the treasure chest, with air bubbles escaping to the top like live pearls. She would fall asleep in front of it, sucking her thumb. Her bedroom was never dark. She was so very afraid of the dark.

'Do you want me to suck you off?'

'No, thank you, Rita. It's kind, but no.'

'With Madeleine then?'

'Not her either. You're both very charming, but no. Let's leave it at that.'

'Well, at least look at us then. That's the least you can do.'

'Okay.'

'It's not that Marco doesn't like women, it's just that he was one once, so he has a chip on his shoulder.'

'*What?*'

'I'll tell you the story. He must have been seventeen or eighteen. He was with three mates in a car going off to a party in some godforsaken corner of Auvergne. All the guys had to dress up as girls, and the girls as guys. Some stupid teenage game, you know. So they go off in their old banger, completely stoned, dressed up to the nines in wigs, miniskirts, high heels, bras and suspenders – the perfect male fantasy. They were having the time of their lives, taking coke and passing around joints. Everything was going great until about nine o'clock, when the car broke down in the middle of nowhere. It was pitch black. There was a little village a couple of miles away and so Marco and one of his friends decided to go and call for help or get a tow. The thing was, they'd forgotten to take a change of clothes, normal clothes, with them. But they had no choice so off they went, hobbling along in their heels, completely off their heads. They arrived at the village only to find that everything was closed – apart from a transport café.

Well, what do you think happened? Two drag queens in a room full of tanked-up knuckleheads, with tattoos like toilet-door graffiti. It was no party, I can tell you. He never really got over it. Something like that must have happened to Gabriel. Everyone's got baggage. Mine is so full I can't even close it.'

'You're still thinking about him, after everything he's done?'

'Of course! When you sleep with one man for so long, even if he's the scum of the earth, at some point you will have seen him hanging on to your breast as if it were a life belt, looking so small, fragile and vulnerable. I know it's stupid, but it's things like that that make you forgive and forget everything. Has that never happened to you?'

'No. I've had the odd fling, but nothing serious. I haven't found The One yet, that's for sure.'

'I'm not talking about finding your one true love. Just love, full stop, the kind that everyone enjoys.'

'No, I don't think I've ever found that either.'

The two women thought he was asleep, curled up on the couch. Madeleine had covered him with a blanket. He had pretended to drift off when they started dancing together and feeling each other up. It was awkward, touching and a little sad. And now they were whispering, one sitting on the pouffe stroking the hair of the other, whose head rested in her lap. A woman's soul is like the Lascaux caves, only older and deeper, so deep that you need a torch, wandering endlessly, leaving handprints, hugging the walls to find your way. Once you enter, there's no way out. You give yourself entirely, getting under her skin to the point that two become one. Madeleine's blanket smelt of her perfume. He would love to drift away down the river, to not exist any more.

'Gabriel? Are you awake? Are you crying?'

A soft hand touched his shoulder, a soft hand heavy with life.

'I was dreaming. What time is it?'

'Does it matter?'

'No, that's just what you say when you wake up, isn't it? Is it morning?'

'Not yet. Do you want a coffee?'

'Yes, please.'

The lovely Madeleine. Her face was as blank as an unwritten letter. Rita was skimming through a book, the sound of the pages passing through her fingers like the fluttering wings of a bird. She stopped at a page and began to read out loud in a voice that wasn't hers: '"I will rise now, and go about the city in the streets, and in the broad ways I will seek him whom my soul loveth: I sought him, but I found him not. The watchmen that go about the city found me: to whom I said, Saw ye him whom my soul loveth?"' Rita closed the book and turned towards the window. Maybe it was the new morning's light on her cheeks, but it looked as though she were crying.

'Isn't it funny – books can really speak to you sometimes. Gabriel, will you help me find Marco?'

You can follow footprints in snow and sand but not in town. The pavements are etched with footsteps, the tarmac is blistered, swollen, dented by them. They come, they go, they leave, they return, walk about, slow down, drag. And then, when their number's up, after a moment's hesitation, they disappear for ever, somewhere, up there.

'We've got to find him, Gabriel! We've got to find him!'

'It's too early, Rita. We can't go and wake the solicitor up now.'

'Why not? Solicitors always get up early; they don't want to miss out on a case.'

'We'll find Marco, but not like this. Not by searching for him. I've got to go and see José.'

'José? What about me?'

'One thing at a time. Go back to Madeleine's, please. You didn't sleep at all last night.'

'Don't talk to me like I'm a kid. You promised me.'

'Rita. I told you I'd help you find Marco and I will. But not now. Later, okay?'

'You're a false saint, Gabriel! That's all you are. You pick us up and then drop us whenever it suits you.'

'Rita! I never said I was a saint! I'm only a man.'

'You're worse than a man. You're an angel – you've got no balls.' Rita aimed a kick at a rubbish bin. Her lizardskin bag swung on the end of her arm like a hammer. She stamped her feet on the pavement; two large tears filled her eyes. Her mouth twisted with rage. She was a balloon ready to burst. 'A miracle? Shit, it's not much to ask, is it?'

And with that she turned on her heel and raced off down the street like a bowling ball. Luckily there was no one in her way.

'Excuse me, sir …'

'Yes?'

'I'd like to open my shop. You're leaning on my shutters.'

'Oh, I'm sorry.'

The man was small and sepia-toned from head to foot. He looked as if he had been born old; or, rather, he was ageless. A mist of a man. For the one thousand and first time he opened the padlock and lifted the shutters just enough to slip into the shop. He reappeared almost immediately armed with a long hooked pole, which he used to push the shutters up fully. Cachoudas Cobblers. The shop's window was decked out with an array of cork-bottomed sandals, sheepskin boots, jars of cream, cans of shoe polish and heels of all sizes; anything and everything to do with feet. A strong smell of glue, leather and rubber drifted through the open door. The cobbler came back into the doorway, buttoning up his overall and taking in one final breath of fresh air. Gabriel was still standing there.

'Were you waiting for me to open? Do you need anything?'

'Yes, some laces.'

'Laces? Come in.'

The shop was so cramped that Gabriel felt the need to shrink in on himself, half dazed by the fumes of glue, sweat and sagging leather. The walls were lined with shelves crammed with boots, ankle boots, loafers, pumps, brogues, ballet slippers and sandals of varying conditions and sizes. They looked like a defeated army. The area behind the counter must have been raised as the small man now towered over Gabriel by a good head. Well, maybe not such a good head. In the light of his anglepoise work lamp, the cobbler's face appeared like that of a severe judge, coldly scrutinising his client.

'Shoelaces. Right then, what kind of shoelaces? There are are all sorts of laces. Short? Long? Rounded? Squared? Thick? Thin? Black? Brown? Red? You've got to give me some idea of the type you're after.'

'Of course. Long ones, please. Round and red.'

'For walking boots?'

'Yes, exactly. For walking boots.'

The man's face lit up. He spread his arms, and the front of his overall gaped between the buttonholes to reveal a brown, clearly hand-knitted jumper beneath.

'Okay then, now we're getting somewhere. Why didn't you say straight away? I've got some Italian ones, virtually in-des-truc-tible. They're here somewhere … hang on.'

Quick as a flash the cobbler disappeared behind his counter and Gabriel remembered that the thing he liked most about puppet shows was the puppeteer. After a good deal of muttering the man reappeared, his face beaming at having found a pair of twisted red laces wrapped in plastic. He held them between thumb and forefinger like a fisherman with his prize catch.

'They're top quality, two-tone but predominantly red. Fifty per cent cotton, fifty per cent silk, resistant to five hundred kilos, and seventy centimetres long. How many do you want?'

'Two of course. I'll take two, a pair.'

'I'd take two pairs if I were you.'

'Ah, but you said they were indestructible.'

'Yes, but you never know. A manufacturing mistake or human error and *bang!* Can you imagine being stuck on a sheer rock face up in the Alps, a shoe falling into the abyss, into a rushing torrent? Night is closing in. You're all alone. You'll regret it.'

'Who said anything about being on a sheer rock face in the Alps at dusk?!'

'Well, everyone ends up there at some time in their life. Believe me, I know! So two pairs then? They're the last ones too. The factory in Modane where they make them is closing down.'

'Oh, really?'

'Yes, it's all nylon and plastic nowadays. It's sad, but that's life. You'll never be able to buy laces like this again.'

'Okay then. I'll take two pairs.'

'Good decision. Are they for somebody special?'

'No.'

'Well, let me wrap them up anyway – they're worth it.'

While the cobbler took his time wrapping the laces in sheets of tissue paper, Gabriel became lost in thought, staring at the dozens of shoes and their dangling labels.

Are we nearly there yet? He marched them up to the top of the hill and he marched them down again. One for the road. Three steps forward, two steps back. Left, right, left, right. These boots were made for walking. Where were they going? Where had they been? Where did they come from?

'Are you looking for someone?'

'Yes, he's a bit of a drifter.'

'What shoe size is he?'

'I don't know. A man, in his forties …'

'Well dressed?'

'Not really. He's a drifter, like I said.'

'Well, in that case he'll definitely drift in here. They all come by at one time or another. There are the straight-laced types in well-fitting boots. Then there are the ones who squeeze their feet into fashionable heels. Even the monks who suffer like martyrs in their new sandals. I've seen them all. It's a bit like a lost-property office for wayward travellers here – the kind who are away with the fairies. What was his name?'

'Marco.'

'Marco, no, I don't recognise the name. I've had a Marcus, Marcus Malte. He made me stick patches on the side of his trainers. You know the kind, an artist! But as for a Marco, no, he's not been in. That'll be €24.40, please.'

Gabriel rummaged through his pockets and pulled out the exact amount.

'Excellent, thank you. The cobbler, you know, is the last stop-off before the desert. If I find your Marco, I'll let you know. Have a good day, sir.'

The doorbell chimed two notes, a *fa* and a *so*.

No, José hadn't hanged himself in the night. He was polishing the counter and serving espressos with the cloth over his shoulder, in the steam of the coffee machine. He had shaved, brushed his hair and was as spotless as a show house. His eyes were dry, too dry.

'Hi there, Gabriel. Surely not a beer at this time in the morning?'

'No, thanks. A coffee.'

José was meticulous in his preparation, mechanical. He was on auto-pilot, but without a plane.

'Are you okay, José?'

'I'm all right. I slept for eighteen hours straight last night. No dreams, no nightmares, just real life, I suppose. How about you?'

'Fine, thanks.'

'Right then, let's go.'

Above the counter, the panda's continued presence demonstrated its ability to be happy everywhere and anywhere.

'I think I'm going to bring her back here.'

'Marie?'

'Yes. She should sleep in her own bed. And, anyway, it'll give me something to do. I need something to do. I feel empty, like there's an echoing cave inside me. I've got to fill it, that's it, I've got to fill it.'

'What about the kids?'

'I'll bring them back as well. It'll be strange for them to start off with, having a mother who sleeps all the time, but they'll be fine. You get used to everything in the end, kids especially. Everything will be nice and peaceful.'

'Being peaceful is good.'

'Yes, it's restful. Hey, I forgot, that guy who sold you the saxophone was in this morning. He was looking for you. He wanted to see you, here, at noon.'

'Ah, thank you. I'll be here. See you later.'

It looked as though the sun had fallen from the sky and shattered like a chandelier on the ground. In the glare, his eyes were whitewashed like the terrace. And then there was the smell, of shit and rotten meat. And the silence, which the buzzing flies served only to accentuate. He clung to the railing with both hands and struggled to breathe. His lungs were tight, gasping for air. His eyes refused to register what they had seen. The space inside his head was filled with the flapping of wings, like tiny black lace fans. Juliette and Blandine lying there, ghostly pale, their faces smeared with dried blood, scribbled over with bluebottles, their blind eyes searching for an answer from the ceiling rose. No, he couldn't believe it. If he did, he could never believe in anything ever again.

The fly sat in the sunbeam as if under a spotlight. It was struggling in a sticky patch on the marble table. It looked like a circus trick gone wrong.

'Thank you for coming, Gabriel.'

Marco held his hand out. It was as cold and slimy as a dead fish.

'Do you want another drink?'

'Yes, please.'

'Waiter, two more coffees. Thanks again for coming. How's Rita?'

'She's looking for you.'

'Ah ...'

Marco leant forward to take a sip, revealing a small bald patch like a monk's on the top of his head. There was a little scar on his scalp in the shape of a half-moon. A childhood accident no doubt, nothing too serious. Marco looked like he'd spent the night on the streets under his raincoat. His pockets were full of tissues and he hadn't shaved. His eyes were bloodshot and his hands were red. There was dirt under his fingernails.

'What have you been up to?'

'I slept in a skip. Do I smell?'

'Not much.'

'How's she doing?'

'She's worried and a bit shaky. But she's being well looked after.'

'She's at 104 Rue Montéléger, third floor on the left, isn't she?'

'How do you know?'

'I followed you. Are you fucking them both?'

'No, neither of them.'

'I don't mind. I'm not jealous. I'm in the shit, Gabriel.'

'What about your inheritance?'

'My inheritance!? I can't get it. My father didn't exactly die of natural causes. I … how would you say … helped him along. Do you remember that night when you came to our room? Well, after you left, I went out. I was off my face on coke, up to my eyeballs; I couldn't sleep. I knew that the old bastard kept some cash at his place. There's no way I was going to settle for just the saxophone. The nurse was sleeping downstairs. I forced open the window and climbed the stairs. I was suffocating in a hat and scarf I'd wrapped round my face. I opened the door to his room. He was stirring in his sleep and snoring like an old locomotive. I didn't think twice about it. I grabbed him by the throat and started hitting him round the head until he told me where he was hiding his loot. I couldn't understand a word he was saying. All that came out of his arsehole of a mouth were disgusting bubbles of spit. I looked for his false teeth, but by the time I'd grabbed them to put in his mouth he'd slipped out of my hands and banged his head on the edge of the bed. Stone-cold dead. Well, just about. He curled into a ball with his fist in his mouth, his knees tucked under his chin. He was naked as the day he was born. He looked like a foetus. He looked like me. I didn't mean to kill him. You've got to understand that, Gabriel. I just wanted to make him talk. I couldn't breathe. I sat on the edge of the bed and cried.'

Marco drank the rest of his coffee in one go and turned the cup round in his hands. He saw no future in the coffee grounds.

'I'd thought about killing him a million times, but I never thought it would turn out like this. I felt completely empty. I had no one left to hate. I was like a boxer, alone in the ring, with just myself to fight against. I felt like an idiot. I rummaged under the mattress and found two bundles of cash. There must have been more but I didn't have the heart to look for them. I gave him one last kick before I left. Yet again, he'd won. And then I went back to the hotel. Rita was fast asleep, snoring. I huddled up against her. I wanted to tell her what had happened but I didn't want to wake her. The next day, well, you know what happened, we went to the restaurant. It was all an act. Rita had too much. I actually thought she was going to overdose on me. I'd had enough of dead people. I packed my bags and took them to the lockers at the station. I wanted to go and see the solicitor and then leave town. On my way over I thought to myself that people might not believe my father had died of natural causes. There was a black car parked outside the solicitor's with four guys inside. I turned round and ran straight ahead, for a long time. This fucking town though, it's tiny. I found myself back where I'd started, the station. It seemed like everywhere I looked there were police. I only had one gram of coke left. I snorted half of it in the toilets. I read everything that people had written on the door. Cries for help. The world's in trouble, serious trouble. My memory gets a bit fuzzy after that. It was as if I was a cocktail shaker in the hands of an epileptic barman. Time flew by like a film on fast forward, an old black and white Charlie Chaplin film. I hung around the hotel and saw you come back and then go out again. I followed you.'

'You should have come up.'

'I thought about it, but didn't dare. I saw your silhouettes in the window. What should I do now?'

'I ... I don't know.'

'Please, help me.'

Marco grabbed Gabriel's wrist. It felt like an ice-cold handcuff. He looked desperately sad and unwell. Gabriel pulled his hand back.

'I think Rita would be very pleased to see you.'

'Yes. I need her. You understand, don't you? She is what she is and I can only be me. We understand each other. Can you get her to meet me? At the station café, perhaps? At about five o'clock?'

'I'll ask her.'

'Thank you. You're a good guy. I'm going to sort myself out. I can't turn up in this state. Okay then, the station café at five it is!'

'Good luck.'

Gabriel munched the rolled-up slice of ham as he walked down the road. It was wrapped, without bread, in a sheet of paper like a crêpe. He hadn't been able to make up his mind in the shop between an egg in aspic, some roast pork and a meat pie. But when the butcher had asked him what he wanted, Gabriel had chosen a slice of ham. It seemed like the easiest thing, neither a good nor bad choice, something in the middle, as bland as blotting paper. They used to give away sheets of blotting paper decorated with Loire Valley châteaux in packets of biscuits. At school, they had learnt to write with a pen dipped in ink, practising upstrokes, downstrokes and blotting the excess. It was strange to think he had once been a child. Of course he remembered, but in the way that you remember an old film: particular sequences in no particular order, insignificant details, a sound, a smell, a quality of light. He remembered the name of a classmate, Brice Soulas. What had happened to

Brice Soulas? And the others, the hundreds, the thousands of others, with whom he had shared a bit of his life. They couldn't all be dead! It wasn't that long ago that he had shaken their hands, hugged them, cried with them, laughed with them and then, suddenly, they'd gone missing in action. Where were they now? Unconsciously, Gabriel began to stare at the passers-by in the absurd hope of discovering a familiar face. After a while he felt as though he knew the people walking past, so much so that when he nodded hello to them they responded. Where were they going?

'Not before the end of the month. Okay. You're welcome.'

Madeleine hung up the phone. She had bags under her eyes, but she was smiling. With her hair tied back and a black silk blouse embroidered with dragons fastened high round her neck, she looked like a madam in 1930s Indochina.

'How are you, Gabriel?'

'Fine, thanks. A bit tired. I'm going to lie down for a while.'

'Let me know if you want anything. It's quiet at the moment.'

'I will, thank you. Oh, by the way, I found Marco. Or, rather, he found me.'

'Marco? Rita's guy?'

'Yes. He wants to see her. He suggested meeting at the station café at five o'clock.'

'He's got some nerve, that one. After dumping her like he did! What does he want to do now? Leave her crying on the station platform? Have you told Rita?'

'No, I thought we could call her. Is she still at yours?'

'I don't like this one bit. He's a dirtbag.'

'That's a bit much. He needs her.'

'Yes, to pimp her out or something! I like Rita a lot; she's a nice girl. She's got the right to a second chance, another life. Marco's no good for her. He's dodgy as hell.'

'José said the same thing and he doesn't even know him.'

'Well, there you go, it's blindingly obvious. He's a bastard, a small-town pimp, a dealer who'd kill his own parents for a hit. AND ... sorry, hang on. Good afternoon, Hôtel de la Gare ... The ninth? Next month? Yes, we've got availability. What's the name? Winter? Like the season? Ah, "tour", okay. Goodbye, Mr Wintour.'

Madeleine hung up and rubbed her temples.

'Where were we? Oh yes. Do we have to tell her? He'll only treat her like shit.'

'It wouldn't be right. Rita's entitled to her say, don't you think?'

'Well, I don't know. How about we go with her to the station? I finish at four o'clock today.'

'I think we should ask her first.'

'I'll call her.'

'Okay, I'm going up. I'll see you later.'

'Blandine? Blandine? Yes, it's me. I can hardly hear you, darling. Yes, I'm fine. How are you? And Juliette? Good, good. Listen, I've missed my plane and there isn't another flight back until tomorrow. A stupid accident on the way to

the airport with the taxi. No, nothing serious, but I missed my plane. No, I know, there's nothing I can do. Is it hot out on the terrace? Yes, same here. I can't wait to see you again. I miss you as well, and Juliette. I'll see you tomorrow. I love you.'

He took a room in the first hotel he saw, next to the airport. It was horrible and expensive, but he couldn't be bothered going back into town. Staying near the airport made him feel closer to home. If it hadn't been for that bloody lorry he would have been home already, on the terrace with a glass of chilled wine in his hand, with his wife, daughter and cats. The neighbour learning the piano would be murdering 'Für Elise', the baby on the other side wailing. Away in the distance he'd watch boats coming and going, their lights reflecting on the port's murky water. The smell of barbecues would linger in the air. They drove like maniacs in this country.

He went down to dinner very early, to get it over with. The restaurant was empty. A row of stressed businessmen hung around the bar, drowning their boredom. They boasted about their successes, winking pathetically at the waitress, who completely ignored them. They looked like a bunch of midgets standing on tiptoes to reach the bar.

Gabriel chewed his mezze absent-mindedly while thinking about the market that he planned to go to with Blandine and Juliette the following Saturday. A haughty woman in her forties came to sit at a nearby table, looking disdainfully about her. She had barely ordered her food before she pulled out a pair of severe-looking glasses and immersed herself in a thick pile of papers. She sat making notes while nibbling at her food, taking small mouthfuls of her fish without looking at what she was eating. All of a sudden, she dropped her fork and pen and began to groan and whimper. She spat into her napkin and clutched her throat. Her cheeks immediately flushed beetroot red. She gulped down half a jug of water to no avail. The fishbone was stuck. She was choking. With no one around to help, Gabriel rushed to her side.

'Eat some bread, not water, some bread.'

The woman was turning a shade of purple, morphing into something unrecognisable. Her bulging eyes, filled with fear as if she were drowning, settled on Gabriel, who was moulding a piece of bread into a small ball. Gurgling noises emerged from her wide-open mouth. Gabriel put the ball of bread in her mouth and indicated to the poor woman that she should try to swallow it. Two more balls of bread were required before she succeeded. Gradually, the woman's panic subsided.

'Is that better?'

'I'm OK, thank you,' she said in English.

Her voice was a bit hoarse, but she had regained her composure. The euphoria of her narrow escape was short-lived. At the sight of her immaculate white shirt now covered in tomato sauce and bits of food she leapt up and grabbed her pile of papers before storming over to the restaurant's entrance where she began to berate the manager in a language he didn't understand.

In the lift back up to his room, Gabriel chuckled to himself, promising to tell the story to Blandine. She loved that kind of thing.

Gabriel didn't tell the story to anyone. He kept it to himself. Now and again he imagined telling Blandine and hearing her laugh.

'I knew you'd find him. You're a really nice guy.'

'It was him who found me. Don't thank me.'

Despite the fact that she was on her third coffee, Rita could barely keep her eyes open. Gabriel and Madeleine had found her asleep on the living-room couch, her mouth open, nostrils quivering, clutching an empty bottle of wine.

'All the same, you're a good guy. Do I look awful?'

Gabriel avoided the question with a vague wave of his hand. He didn't want to tell her she looked as battered and creased as the pillow she had collapsed on. Madeleine paced up and down the room, her arms crossed, failing to contain her fury.

'You look shocking, just like you did when that bastard left you on your own at the hotel!'

'Have I got time to take a shower?'

'Yes, you've got time, but, Rita, listen to me, that man

will be the death of you! I'm sorry, but I can't stand seeing you go running after him as soon as he reappears. You're a woman; you've got your dignity.'

'Dignity? Madeleine, you've got to understand that Marco needs me. He's the only person who has always needed me. It's important to feel useful, you know, even if it is to somebody like Marco. I'm not stupid, I know what he's like.'

'Go and take your shower. We're coming with you though. Are you still okay with that?'

'Of course. I'd like you to be there. You can both be my witnesses. It's crazy – I'm as excited as a bride on her wedding day!'

Madeleine shrugged her shoulders and rolled her eyes as Rita scurried off to the bathroom humming *La Vie en Rose*. It was like being on the set of a farce: doors opened, doors closed. Gabriel made the most of the interval to have a look out at the street. It must lead somewhere, mustn't it? On to another street, leading on to another street, leading on ...

'Witnesses! To a duel, in fact! What do you think, Gabriel?'

'Witnesses are important. They're not just bit-parts. You need them.'

'I'm not talking about that! I'm thinking of Rita. He's going to take advantage of her! And we're just going to stand there. You're not just going to let her go off with that—'

'I think I am. They love each other.'

'You call that *love?* I call it "failure to render assistance to a person in danger". It'll end in disaster.'

'And?'

'What do you mean "and"? You can't just let people kill themselves without trying to do something!'

'Why not?'

'Because you just can't; it's wrong.'

'You're jealous of her, aren't you?'

'*Me?* Absolutely not! I feel sorry for her.'

'You shouldn't do. She's worth much more than that. Tell me, the road outside your house, which street does it lead on to?'

'Rue Chaptal. Why?'

'I've not been down there yet. I should take a look.'

Rita charged ahead like a Russian tank, fuelled by vodka and driven by an irrepressible urge to conquer the void. She had the bodywork as well: leather and jeans festooned with zips, carefully spiked hair, pointy breasts, and crêpe-soled shoes like tyre treads.

'Of course I won't, Madeleine. I won't throw myself at him. I want an apology first. After that, we'll see.'

'Gabriel and I aren't going to let you out of our sight. Let us know if you want us to step in.'

'It'll be fine. How do I look? Do I look rough?'

Gabriel brought up the rear. The two women in front of him were an invincible team, like breakers sweeping forward. Soon they were at the station with its disappointing view. The small panes of its windows strained to reflect the dull light of a cracked sky at the end of a gloomy day. The square was now no more than an enormous hole surrounded by wire fences, at the bottom of which diggers churned up the earth while little men in yellow hard hats attempted to create, out of the chaos, the world's greatest car park. It looked like a dig in Egypt. The café modestly offered its humble purgatory to all passing waifs and strays ... Rita peered in through the window.

'There he is. He looks depressed.'

'You go in first. Gabriel and I will sit near the entrance. Don't let him walk all over you.'

From where they were sitting, Madeleine and Gabriel had a pretty good view of them, Rita from the back and Marco from the side. Even shaved and wearing clean clothes, Marco looked in the same sad state as he had done that morning. Rita shunned Marco's outstretched hand with a simple shake of her head. Crushed, Marco stared at his spurned hand. He looked as if he wanted to wrench his arm off and throw it over his shoulder. Gabriel and Madeleine couldn't hear what they were saying, but Marco's body language, his head shrunk back in his jacket collar, showed that he was ready to take the blame, to accept his fate. He would just have to wait for it to pass. And it did pass. Now it was Rita who took his hands and held them in hers. He smiled and Rita leant towards him.

'Here we go! I don't know what she sees in him. He's ugly as sin. Personally, I—'

A gust of air hit them as two strapping men entered and made straight for the row of tables where Marco and Rita were sitting. Marco turned ashen, his eyes widened and his mouth dropped open at the sight of the pair of heavies who wore official red armbands. They appeared to be going for Marco, but, instead, laid their paws on the shoulders of another man sitting at the table behind. The whole episode was over in just a few seconds. The two policemen hauled the man off his seat and dragged him out of the café, while the stunned customers looked on. Marco's hand went to his chest and he collapsed forward onto the table. Rita leapt up and started screaming.

'Marco! Marco!'

A large moustachioed man, for some reason dressed in lederhosen, rushed over.

'I'm a doctor.'

There was mayhem. People were getting out of their seats, rushing to the toilets or taking advantage of the confusion to slip off without paying. Others crowded around Rita and Marco. The doctor loosened Marco's tie and took his pulse, while Rita watched, distraught.

'Is he dead?'

'No, but he's had a heart attack. We need to call an ambulance.'

The waiters waved white flags. The war was over.

'Jesus, really? Where is he?'

'In intensive care. They think he'll pull through.'

'Well, at least it proves he's got a heart.'

José stared at the counter he had just finished wiping. A barely visible mark had caught his attention. He scrubbed it with the corner of the cloth.

'Damned thing won't budge!'

'What is it?'

'Glue, I think.'

'You can't really see it.'

'I can. Anyway, I'm going to go and pick up the kids tomorrow. Françoise is going to live with us for a bit, so she can help out.'

'And Marie?'

'When everything is ready, at the end of the week, then maybe. I can't be by myself any more. I'm sick of my own company. What on earth *is* this?'

José couldn't stand it any longer. He took a penknife from his pocket and started scratching at the tiny translucent mark.

'There we go. It looks like a contact lens.'

José balanced the shiny item on the end of his finger like a hat and held it out to Gabriel.

'Yes, definitely a contact lens.'

'Weird thing to find on a bar. I'll put it to one side in case the owner comes back for it.'

Under the benevolent eye of the panda, watching over the world with constant cheer, José rummaged through a drawer in search of a matchbox in which to store the lens. Gabriel noted that whenever José passed close to the toy he made sure to touch its paw, tummy or nose. St Panda?

'What are you doing tonight, José?'

'Nothing, obviously.'

'I'm cooking at Madeleine's. Rita needs cheering up. Would you like to come along?'

'No, thanks. I'm not really in the mood.'

'You're allowed to enjoy yourself, once in a while.'

'I know, but … Is Rita really unhappy then?'

'Pretty unhappy, yes.'

'Ah.'

José rubbed his stubbled cheeks, staring at the panda. Unhappy people had to stick together.

'Okay then. Where does she live?'

'Just round the corner, 104 Rue Montéléger, third floor on the left. By the way, do you know if there's an Italian deli round here?'

'There's the Stromboli. It's a restaurant, but you can

buy things to take away. It's on Rue Chaptal.'

Rue Chaptal was a dead end in more ways than one. The scars of long-gone shops ran along its length: hardware shops, a horse-meat butcher's, a haberdashery now reduced to rusty signs with letters missing. Apart from the string of multicoloured light bulbs around the Stromboli's window, the street was in darkness.

'We're not open for dinner yet.'

'I was just after a few bits and pieces, fresh pasta, that kind of thing.'

With a show of regret the woman, who had a strong German accent, put a bookmark in her copy of *Also Sprach Zarathustra*, and rose to her full six feet. Her bobbed platinum hair was like a helmet, the fringe finishing just above her steel-blue eyes.

'What kind of pasta?'

'Tagliatelle.'

'For how many people?'

'Four.'

The woman put on a pair of latex gloves and filled a small bag with the pasta. Between her powerful fingers, the ribbons looked peculiarly like sauerkraut.

'Anything else?'

'Some Parma ham, please. Twenty or so slices, very thin.'

The leg of ham was almost whole, but looked weightless in the woman's hands. The meat slicer buzzed unnervingly as the twenty slivers piled up on one another.

'Anything else?'

'A tub of pesto, a packet of breadsticks and I could do with some antipasti, some artichokes in oil, roasted peppers. I'm sorry, but I go a bit mad when I'm in an Italian deli. I just want to take everything.'

'I know. I was like that ten years ago.'

The woman got Gabriel to try everything before packing it into tubs. She told him her story.

'I was on an architecture field trip to Florence. There was a little shop right next door to my hotel. It was dirty, dark and reeked of faraway spices, cheese and cured meat. It smelt of men. It took me four days to pluck up the courage and give in to temptation. The man who cut me five slices of coppa was called Adamo and naturally he was gorgeous. Like mine, his father was dead, and had been a fascist. We were made for each other. Adamo wanted to travel and I had some money saved up. The rest is history. Will that be all?'

'Have you got any Lacryma Christi?'

'Yes.'

'I'll take two bottles then, please. That's a great story. So what made you choose to set up shop here?'

'We wanted to go far away. This was the perfect place.'

'Do you like it here?'

'No, but "what doesn't kill me makes me stronger" as Nietzsche once said.'

'That's true. My compliments to the chef – the antipasti are delicious.'

Gabriel had barely finished speaking before the woman pressed a button and a distant-sounding voice crackled out of a loudspeaker.

'*Prego?*'

'Adamo, a customer wants to pass on his compliments for the antipasti.'

'*Grazie! Grazie mille, grazie tanti, grazie mille, graz*—'

'Okay, okay. Have a nice evening, sir.'

'You too.'

Gabriel left the shop, convinced that the voice coming out of the loudspeaker was a broken record, stuck on '*Grazie! Grazie mille.*'

It wouldn't come, no matter how much he needed to go. Piss, just piss. It wasn't rocket science. Even a newborn baby knew instinctively how to piss. But it just wouldn't come. This appendage hanging out of his flies would end up useless. It didn't look bad, not too long, not too short, silky smooth, good girth, nice shape, no spots or shrivelling. The toilet he was standing in front of looked like a pelican made of white china, its beak open, waiting patiently for his thing to recover from its momentary bout of amnesia. The sound of clinking cutlery, soft background music and the hubbub of conversation drifted through from the other side of the closed door. Life could obviously go on without him. At that exact moment, only the sunfish in the postcard pinned to the wall above the cistern could vouch for his existence. And it wasn't helping. The fully inflated creature, bristling with spikes, reminded him of his bladder.

'Come on then – are you or aren't you?'

Annoyed, he waved it around in every direction, but soon came to the conclusion that violence never got you anywhere. The more you want something, the further you push it away.

Okay then, he thought to himself, let's pretend we're here to do something else: to study the sunfish's morphology perhaps, or even to test the quality of the toilet paper. It's a good brand, thick and soft. Count the tiles on the floor. Twenty, two with bevelled corners. The journey into the afterlife promised to be thrilling.

'Right, come on. I've had enough,' he muttered to himself.

Disappointed, he tucked himself back in and, out of principle, flushed the toilet. The sound of the rushing water aroused something in his abdomen. Suddenly, he felt an urgent need and everything started all over again.

'Are you all right in there, Gabriel?'

'Fine, thanks. I'll be out in a second.'

There was not an olive nor a morsel of pasta left on their plates. Despite the grief and the sorrow, they had been hungry. The two bottles of Lacryma Christi had been drunk. Thankfully, José had brought another two bottles of wine. Rita and he were getting on well. They were all taking comfort from each other. Unhappy people were part of the same big happy family. Rita had shown José the photo of her white poppy and he had shown her a photo of his family in happier times.

Madeleine watched them tenderly, her head resting on her hand, her elbow on her knee. Which sea was she daydreaming about? How deep was she swimming?

Everything should stop here, now, when everything was perfect. It should be like this for ever. Gabriel wanted to be able to persuade them to stay as they were, not to move a muscle, not to say another word. Because he knew. He knew. He had been here once before, that day on the terrace, the heat, the closed shutters, Blandine enjoying a siesta, the cats at her feet, a fly buzzing, Juliette in her hammock, the piano playing, the baby wailing, the ferry's whistle, the smell of the barbecue and the melon skin. That day he hadn't known. He should never have left the next day. The first one to move would break the charm. Their bubble would burst.

'Hey, Gabriel. Gabriel. Are you with us? I was just telling them the story of the panda.'

'Ah, yes, the panda.'

They already had memories in common, some good and some bad. Rita looked younger; there was something childlike about her, as if she had cried herself clean.

'It's funny. It's as though you've known each other since school.'

'If it wasn't for the couple of hundred miles between us, then maybe. Having said that, when the two of you came to my restaurant the other night, I thought you and Madeleine were sisters.'

'No, I could never stand my brothers and sisters. Anyway, that doesn't matter. We're here now, together. You get the family you deserve.'

Gabriel blinked; on, off, on, off. Anyone can feel like family in the end; you just have to replace the smiling faces in the identikit photo.

The thing that had struck Gabriel was how young they were. One was sixteen and the other seventeen. They had stood there, like bored schoolchildren, half listening to a lecture on discipline. They were probably thinking about the football match that the judge was making them miss. They had confessed to everything on their arrest. A fuck-up. It wasn't their fault if someone had told them to burgle the wrong flat. They had got the wrong door. Shit happens. They were stoned and it was late. They'd panicked when the woman and child started screaming – you know how it is. They were sorry. They would never do it again. They promised. They swore. Their past had been lousy; all they cared about now was the telly and the football score between Les Bleus and Italy. They agreed to pay the price for their youthful error. Fifteen years, five suspended, ten years in prison. They would still be young when they got out. Whether they spent those years on the inside or out made little difference. With their shaved heads, sticking-out ears, brand-new tracksuits and trainers, they looked like young sportsmen apologising after an unfortunate defeat: 'We'll do better next time.'

As hard as he tried, Gabriel couldn't bring himself to hate them. Even before meeting them, even before knowing who had done it, the enormity of the crime had stripped bare his sense of good and evil. It was like a natural disaster, a volcanic eruption, a tsunami, an earthquake, something beyond all comprehension. His lawyer and family were surprised, if not dismayed, by his lack of fighting spirit. They wanted him to show hate, a thirst for vengeance, but Gabriel had none. He had tried to imagine gouging out the eyes of his wife and child's torturers, but he couldn't manage it. Curiously, he felt he had more in common with the guilty pair than with his friends as, like him, the two boys failed to feel the difference between good and evil. He would rather watch the final with them. Like them, he had nothing left to say for himself. The guilty one, the real one, was still on the run. The one without name or form that humanity invoked every day. He would never be troubled.

They heard a roar from outside the courtroom. France were leading 1–0. Lawyers, murderers, victims and judges joined in a silent cheer.

José had drunk a fair amount and, although he struggled to get up off the couch, he managed to stand up without swaying.

'I have to go. I'm getting up early tomorrow.'

Tomorrow ... Madeleine resurfaced from her reverie. Rita rubbed her eyes and Gabriel looked down.

Rita poured the last dregs of wine into her glass and finished it in one.

'So then, it's all over.'

José blushed as if caught out. His eyes searched in vain for something to hold on to. He felt guilty. It wasn't easy playing Judas. He stared down at his feet as if they were made of lead.

'All good things must come to an end.'

'Why?'

'Because if they don't then you won't realise how good they've been. That's just the way it is, can't be helped.'

Rita fell back onto the couch with a sigh, her arm held

over her eyes. Madeleine started to clear the table. Gabriel got up and offered his hand to José, who grabbed it as one would a life belt.

'Well, that's life, isn't it?'

'*C'est la vie*. Goodnight, José. By the way, can I come along with you tomorrow?'

'If you want. We'll all squeeze in.'

Madeleine offered him her spineless sunfish cheek. Rita didn't move from the couch. She was sleeping, or at least pretending to. José hesitated as he leant over to kiss her goodnight. He pulled back.

'So then, I'll see you tomorrow.'

'Goodnight, José.'

Madeleine emptied the ashtrays full of dreams while Gabriel opened a window. The party spirit swirled out and dissolved in the rectangle of velvety darkness like fine drizzle evaporating. Madeleine joined Gabriel at the window.

'I've drunk too much.'

They both leant against the windowsill, as though holding on to a ship's rail as it pulled out of harbour. The street was quiet.

'Have you ever been happy, Gabriel?'

'Yes, once. It frightened me.'

'Why?'

'Because it was the last time.'

'I don't know if I should envy you or feel sorry for you.'

'Neither.'

'You're going to leave, aren't you?'

'Of course, like everybody else.'

'To go where?'

'I don't know. Somewhere like this probably.'

'So why don't you stay?'

'It's not up to me.'

Below, on the opposite pavement, a blind man walked by. He would have passed by unnoticed if it hadn't been for the tippy-tappy sound of his white stick. The sound of a shadow.

'What about him? Do you think he knows where he's going?'

'Definitely. A blind man's at home in darkness.'

'This evening, everybody was happy – José, Rita. But you weren't. What's stopping you from being happy?'

'I'm not unhappy.'

'I love you, Gabriel. It's stupid, but it's true.'

The blind man turned a corner. The sound of his stick gradually faded away before disappearing completely. The town lay still, bathing in dreams in which everybody was a hero. He had to sleep. Sleep.

'I'm going back to the hotel, Madeleine. It's late.'

She'd never been as beautiful as she was then. Much more beautiful than her geranium.

'That's a nice gun you've got there, Françoise.'

'It belonged to my husband. He was a great hunter. I clean it regularly. It's in perfect condition, like when he was alive.'

The little girl resembled a wild strawberry trampled by an elephant. Her small hand still gripped the saxophone with which she had just played a flawless, if slightly fast, rendition of *Au Clair de la Lune* for Gabriel. Beside her, as if asleep, her brother sat leaning against the wall, his arms slack by his sides, his legs extended, his chin resting on his chest, in the middle of which the buckshot had left a hole the size of an orange. Françoise lay in the hallway, a few feet from the door. She was faceless, as if a mask had been ripped violently off her. José was at the foot of the stairs on his back, his arms outstretched, his mouth wide open and his eyes burning with shock. The echo of the last gunshot still rang in the stairwell. José had been halfway up the stairs when he saw Gabriel on the landing with the gun in his hand.

'Gabriel? What on earth—'

The force of the gunshot blew him away.

Gabriel stepped over José's body, put the gun on the kitchen table and filled a large glass with tap water. The smell of gunpowder had dried his mouth. Everything had happened so quickly, two minutes at most.

Happiness is a calamity you can never recover from. As soon as you catch a glimpse of it, the door slams shut and you spend the rest of your life bitterly regretting what is no more. There is no worse purgatory and no one knew that better than Gabriel. The Westminster clock struck eleven, immortalising the moment for ever. He felt vacant and hollow, his bones and arteries empty, as if all the blood that had been spilt had been his own. He was hungry and wanted a beer. That was what the two kids had done after they had torn his family apart. They had gone and plundered his fridge and drunk some beers. That must be the normal reaction. His path back to the car was strewn with abandoned luggage.

It was always like that with the horizon: you never knew where it really ended. There had to be a hole in it, that was it, an unending chasm. And the sky. It has to break into day, but you sense that it doesn't really want to. It's a sky that would rather go back to bed.

Gabriel parked the car on the roadside. He had a pressing urge. His jet of urine swept over the wild grass and unnamed indestructible plants. Once a year they blossomed, producing scrawny and charmless flowers as well as seeds, which allowed them to reproduce. All for nothing. They weren't edible and would never look good in a bouquet. Like humanity, a lot of creation is totally pointless. And yet it is this kind of landscape that is the most resistant. You could piss on it for ever.

As he closed his flies, Gabriel's gaze was drawn to the clump of brambles opposite. Despite its apparent chaos, there seemed to him to be a deep-rooted architectural logic to this tangle of barbed branches. It wasn't just coincidence that one stalk had wound itself round another three times. Nothing was left to chance. Everything happened for a reason. It was fascinating. The icy wind blew its foul breath in his face. Gabriel felt tired. He climbed back into the car, tipped the seat back and turned on the radio. The presenter was telling a stupid joke but it made him laugh. A man walks into a bar ...

The space outside the Faro where José had been parked that morning was still empty. Gabriel pulled up, cut the engine and closed his eyes. He remembered the big brasserie at the end of the street where the two young businessmen had argued over the babies' bottles and their mismatched teats. Sauerkraut, that's what he wanted. A good plate of sauerkraut.

'What are you doing, Rita?'

'I'm cooking an egg, can't you see?'

Her face was swollen. She wore a baggy tracksuit and dirty slippers. With her arms folded in front of the stove, she stared into the pan of boiling water, watching the egg dance from side to side. Everything seemed too big for her, her skin, her clothes, her life. The little girl with the white poppy was once again forgotten in the purse at the bottom of the bag. She had the same air of resignation as José had had that morning when picking up his kids, his neck stretched out to take the yoke of a life already written and planned in advance. A look that said every day was like a Monday morning.

'José lent me his car. I was thinking, I could take you to the hospital if you want.'

'Um, yeah, I guess so. Only if you want.'

'It is today you're going, isn't it?'

'Yes, yes. I'll eat my egg and then we can go. The coffee's still hot if you want some.'

The dishes from the night before had been washed and stacked precariously in the drainer. Opposite Gabriel, Rita carefully peeled the shell off her egg. Once finished, she took her time looking at the egg before taking a bite. The coffee was lukewarm.

'What time is it?'

'Twenty past three.'

'I didn't sleep a wink last night. How are José and the kids? And their grandmother?'

'They're fine.'

'Good. He's nice, José, not complicated, not needy. He doesn't ask for much.'

'Have you heard anything from Marco?'

'I called the hospital this morning. They didn't want to give me any details. He's not dead though. Right, I'll put some clothes on and then we can go.'

'You've got a bit of egg yolk in the corner of your mouth.'

'Ah, thank you.'

Warehouses and retail parks selling all sorts of useless tat sprouted on the edge of town, amid the turn-offs and roundabouts. They were all overburdened with signs, logos and giant arrows shouting 'Come on in! This is where it's at!' But actually finding the entrance was always a nightmare. A windscreen wiper squeaked annoyingly.

'Pull over at that café there. I have to get a drink before the hospital.'

The supermarket café was full of people coming and going. But they could all have been the same person, more or less successfully disguised, with moustaches, glasses, wigs or shaved heads. Rita was already on her third beer She wasn't talking, preferring instead to smoke and chew her fingernails, her gaze drifting towards the car park full of puddles.

'Are you worried, Rita?'

'No, it's not that. I'm fed up with going nowhere. I feel like I've been pedalling just to stay still my entire life. José's got his kids, a family …'

'You've got Marco.'

'Yes, or maybe he has me. I've been a whore for him and now I can be his nurse! When happiness doesn't come, there's nothing you can do about it. Last night was good though, wasn't it?'

'Yes, it was good.'

'At least that's something. Let's go.'

The hospital wasn't that different from the shopping centre. It was also a cube-shaped block, probably dreamt up by the same architect, but with stretchers instead of shopping trolleys, humans instead of groceries. Here, as at the supermarket, business was good. Gabriel struggled to find a place to park. Rita fidgeted in her seat.

'Gabriel, let's get out of here.'

'Hold on, it's fine, I'll find a space. Look, there's one over there.'

'Let's go, I said! I don't want to go inside. Let's get out of here!'

'If that's what you want. Where do you want to go?'

'Anywhere, I don't care. Let's go.'

Rita's cheeks were red and glazed with tears, which she let run down her face without wiping them away. She sniffled, her lower lip sticking out dejectedly. Gabriel drove around aimlessly, a left turn here, a right turn there. They drove through a small estate full of new houses, all identical, reproduced ad infinitum. Past that, they travelled through fields, all flat except for the odd cluster of bare trees. Rita's tears had dried up. Her breathing was back to normal. She dabbed her eyes and blew her nose.

'I'm sorry, Gabriel, but I just couldn't.'

'You don't need to apologise.'

'Can you pull up here by the trees? I need to pee. Those beers ...'

Gabriel turned off down a rutted dirt track and cut the engine. Rita jumped out of the car. Through the wet windscreen he could see her scrambling through the undergrowth and then suddenly disappearing into a thicket. One day, he had taken Juliette to the mountains to see the marmots. Every time he had pointed one out to her, the animal had disappeared down a hole before she had managed to see it. They returned home with Juliette convinced that it had all been one big joke. As far as she was concerned, marmots didn't exist.

Without thinking, Gabriel started playing with one of the laces he had bought at the cobbler's. He wound it round his hand and tested its resistance by pulling on it. The rain started hammering on the roof. Rita ran back to the car and jumped in, her hair flattened by the rain.

'Fucking mud! My shoes got bloody stuck in it. I've got

mud up to my knees. I hate the countryside.'

Rita brushed her hair back, slumped into the seat, closed her eyes and sighed.

'My God, it feels good to take a piss when you really need one. It's nice hearing the rain, when you're under cover ...'

Rita wasn't as heavy as he had thought. But these brambles catching at his clothes, and the slippery mud ... He got to the spot where he thought he had seen her crouch. Her face was calm, peaceful. The rain washed away her tear-smudged make-up. She hadn't struggled when Gabriel had leant in. Maybe she thought he wanted to kiss her. It was only by reflex that she had stretched her legs and arms out as the lace tightened round her neck.

'... I never left the apartment. I didn't answer the phone, pick up my mail or answer the doorbell. I spent my days lying on the terrace looking at the sky. It was still just as blue, the kind of blue you can get lost in. And then one day I got up from my deckchair and shut the door behind me. I took only what I could carry on my back. I think I caught a ferry or a train, I can't remember. Once the door had shut I started to forget. The days and nights merged into one. I slept wherever and whenever I could. With each day that passed, I forgot a little more of myself. I wandered around Paris for a bit. I could have chosen anywhere, but I chose Paris. Perhaps because I was born there and wanted to go back to where it had all started, or perhaps it was just to disappear into the crowd. It was cold. When I was so drunk I couldn't sleep, I would walk until I started to hallucinate. It was like that every day. Always the same. I couldn't feel anything, except the weight of my tiredness, and that's all I wanted. One night I got picked up half frozen off a pavement. I woke up in hospital. I don't know how but my friends found out. I asked them to sell everything I owned, the house, the car, everything, and then not to come searching for me ever again. I never wanted to go back, ever. After I left the hospital I went into a convalescent home. I stayed there for weeks, months, until one day I felt a sudden urge to see the sea. I needed something to look at other than the walls of my room. I felt trapped. I needed space, to be far away. I got the first train to Brest. Don't ask me why – I couldn't tell you. I was suffocating in the train carriage. I needed air. That's the whole story.'

The headlights from the cars travelling in the opposite direction flashed across Madeleine's face. Since Gabriel had started telling his story, she had gone rigid, as milky-white and transparent as an alabaster statue.

'Why are you telling me this now?'

'Because we're alone in a car at night. Let me know if you want to stop to eat or drink something.'

'No. I can't take it all in. Rita, José, you … You've all been through so much. And I'm just floating through it all, oblivious …'

'I'm sorry, I shouldn't have said anything.'

'Of course you should. It's always good to talk.'

'I don't know. I've never spoken about it to anyone. My suffering has stopped though. It's just the pain of others which hurts me. I always want to help them.'

'You're very good at it. You've been great to José, and Rita as well.'

'But not you?'

'Oh, you can forget about me. I've never been too happy or too sad, just bored. You get used to it. I'm so happy to have met you and to be here with you now in this car, tonight.'

'It's lucky you were able to get away for a couple of days.'

'My boss owed me! I had so much holiday to take. What else was I going to do with it? It was fine. It was kind of José to lend you his car.'

'It was him who suggested it. He said, "You're looking after me and Rita too much and you're neglecting Madeleine. Borrow the car and take her to the sea."'

'What a great idea! It's just that I'm a bit worried about Rita.'

'Don't be. When she reads your note, she'll understand. She was fine, really, when I dropped her off at the hospital.'

'So we've got clear consciences then?'

'Absolutely. What time is it?'

'It's just gone quarter past eight.'

'We'll be at Roscoff in half an hour. I hope there'll be a restaurant still open.'

'There's bound to be a crêperie.'

'I hope so. I'm hungry. Here we are at Morlaix.'

Road signs lit up by their headlights flashed by: Saint-Martin-des-Champs, Sainte-Sève, Taulé, Saint-Pol-de-Léon … They were just signposts, that was all. Nothing was there to prove that these places actually existed. The night dissolved these villages like sugar in coffee. You passed them by without seeing them and forgot them almost as quickly: a high street, a war memorial, a town hall, a post office, a church, a graveyard and it was over. You moved on to the next one.

'Why did you choose the Île de Batz, Gabriel?'

'Because you can walk all the way round it in a morning.'

'Gabriel, look at this shell – it's huge!'

Blandine was running over to him holding something in her hand that looked from a distance like a skull. Her yellow raincoat was the only splash of colour in an otherwise pearly-grey landscape. He was scared she would slip on the green and brown algae-covered rocks. The wind carried his voice away, so he signalled to her to be careful. But she took no notice. She leapt over rock pools in the oversized wellington boots they had borrowed from the hotel. Her momentum carried her into Gabriel's arms and the two of them fell onto the sand. She smelt of salt and of the breeze. The shell looked like a big ear. She put it up to her ear, then up to Gabriel's and then held it against her already round stomach.

'Listen to that, Juliette. It's the Breton sea. Your mummy and daddy are there right now. Do you want to say something? I'll pass you over.'

The sea grunted. It was grumpy that day. The drizzle made their mouths slippery.

'Darling, build us an island in the sun!'

And he did.

It was still dark when they left the hotel. Apart from the wind whistling, the streets were empty. There were only a few lights on, one at the baker's where they had bought croissants, and a neon sign belonging to the bar by the pier where they sought shelter from the rain lashing against the austere facades of the blank houses. Madeleine stirred her hot chocolate in a daydream, smiling like the panda. Gabriel chewed his croissant while watching the raindrops slide down the dark pane of glass. Besides the owner, there were two other people in the bar: a tall red-haired man with a moustache who was speaking English, and an old woman dressed in tweed and fur-lined boots, who looked very dignified, her white hair pulled back into a tight bun. The old woman sipped a cup of tea and stared absent-mindedly at the row of bottles above the bar. From time to time he made chit-chat about the weather or unknown people with John, the owner. There was a smell of stuffy bedrooms, cosy duvets and morning coffees in the air.

'Gabriel?'

'Yes?'

'Nothing. I feel good.'

Madeleine placed her hand on Gabriel's. She had said it without smiling, as if it was something serious, something solemn.

'Me too,' he replied.

'Do you regret it?'

'What?'

'Us two, last night?'

'Not at all — the opposite actually. Was I okay? It's been such a long time.'

'It would have been great even if we hadn't done it.'

After eating some excellent seafood pancakes at the crêperie they had gone back to the hotel. They had taken turns in the shower and then lain on the bed watching TV, enjoying a mindless game show. Looking at them, you would have thought they had spent their lives together. In the end, they had turned the light off and made love simply and quickly with all the awkwardness of first-timers.

'There's the boat.'

John pointed to the squat outline of a boat arriving from Île de Batz in the first light of dawn, walnut-sized on the horizon. The old woman got up and put on a long green raincoat and a rain hat. She wasn't particularly tall, but with her fixed gaze she seemed to dominate everything around her, like a lighthouse.

It was hard to stay upright walking along the jetty, with the wind charging at them like a battering ram. The old lady walked in front of them, head straight, indifferent. Two men helped them onto the boat. The three passengers went and sat inside on wooden benches. It was like being back at school, packed in, their arms crossed. The waves rocked them from side to side, shoulder to shoulder.

Under the lowering sky, the Île de Batz appeared, a naked shoulder emerging from the sea. The crossing had only taken fifteen minutes but long after they had set foot on land the boat's pitching remained in their legs.

'Which way, left or right?'

'It doesn't matter. An island is like a beret — there's no right way.'

'Let's go left then.'

'Why?'

'We write from left to right and for me today is a blank page.'

They weren't really villages, just clusters of houses and place names – Kenekaou, Porz Kloz – separated from one another by creeks, dunes, moors and fields. It took them just half an hour to reach the island's easterly tip and a botanical garden. It was an island within an island, an exotic oasis where palm trees grew as if back home under sunnier climes. A ray of sunlight breaking through the clouds shone like a spotlight on the leaves of the rubber, yucca and other plants with unpronounceable names. A tern landed on a palm tree in front of Madeleine.

'It's unbelievable. This is paradise. That's what it is, paradise!'

'I know. Are you coming?'

Blandine had said exactly the same thing, in exactly the same place, ten years earlier.

Side by side, stooping into the wind, they followed the smugglers' path, the sea on their right shaking its petticoat tails in a breathtaking can-can.

'Let's sit down here for a moment.'

Down below, pink granite boulders were jumbled on top of each other, making the shapes of bizarre animals in the process of transformation.

'See that one? It looks like a tortoise. And that one over there looks like a sad dog. And over there—'

'You know what this place is called?'

'No.'

'The Snake's Hole. Legend has it that it was here that St Pol killed a dragon which was terrorising the island's inhabitants. If you lean over the side and listen carefully to the waves, it sounds like laughter. Listen.'

Madeleine inched tentatively forward.

'It must be terrifying here when there's a storm.'

'Terrifying.'

'But with you I'm not scared of anything. If you only knew how happy I am, to be here with you between the sea and the sky. You can't get any happier than this.' She paused. 'Gabriel, what's wrong?'

At the foot of the hole the water whirled, lapping hungrily against the rocks. *You can't get any happier than this.*

'Gabriel? What are you doing?'

They were high up, very high. All it would take was one small dancing step, the half-turn of a waltz, and Madeleine, like José, like Rita, like the others, would be happy ever after.

'Gabriel, you're holding me too tight; you're hurting me.'

And the waves below applauded. They applauded.

'And what would you like to drink with the crab? A white wine perhaps?'

'Yes, please.'

'And a jug of water, please.'

'Of course, Madame.'

The romantic Bernique was the only restaurant that was open on the island. They had a choice of crab or ... crab. They were enormous, the size of tanks. Madeleine fiddled with the surgical tools to extract the white meat from the creature lying open in front of her, claws hanging off the plate. Gabriel, his eyes half closed, watched her through the swirling smoke of his cigarette.

'They're enormous! I don't know where to start.'

'Do you want me to crack the claws for you?'

'Yes, please.'

Gabriel got to work using a nutcracker-like tool, itself in the form of a crab claw.

'You know, earlier, at the Snake's Hole, it's stupid but I thought you were going to push me in.'

'Really? Why would I have done that?'

'I don't know. You were holding on to me so hard and we were so close to the edge. Your eyes were empty, like the drop behind me.'

Gabriel hadn't been able to. Madeleine had reached the peak of her happiness, and would never make it up there again. Anything else would only be a slow and tedious decline. To finish her at the height of her happiness and in water, her favourite element, too, seemed like a no-brainer. But he couldn't do it. His hands had relinquished their grip on her shoulders and fallen limply by his side. His head was ringing with the roar of the sea from the hole, that swirl of foaming green jelly, indignant that it had been refused its ration. Madeleine had quickly taken two steps forward and rubbed her shoulders, staring ahead, open-mouthed.

'Let's go, Gabriel.'

'Yes ... yes, of course. Are you hungry?'

They had reached the restaurant without having said a word to each other.

Four locals, their caps pulled down low over their eyes, were playing cards at a table near the entrance. Depending on how the game was going, they let out onomatopoeic grunts and groans. It was impossible to hold a conversation, even a boring one, and shell a crab at the same time. Like the belote players, Gabriel and Madeleine spoke only in sucking noises, chewing sounds and the occasional sharp crack. Their tray was now littered with shell shrapnel and crumpled balls of lemon-scented hand wipes.

'What time's the boat?'

'Five, I think.'

'And then what?'

'What do you mean?'

'Once we get to the other side?'

'And then …'

The boat had barely set sail and already the island had faded in the distance. Only a few twinkling lights remained on the skyline. They hadn't noticed it getting dark. It was difficult to keep your balance, even gripping the handrail, as the round-bottomed boat was thrown about by the waves. Even so, Madeleine was determined to stay on deck. It smelt of salt and tar.

'It feels like the island only existed today, for us. I'm never going back.'

She said this without sadness or regret. It was what it was … 'I'm never going back.'

'Excuse me, could you please return below deck? It's too dangerous out here in this weather.'

José's car was waiting for them on the quayside. Loyal. Resigned.

'Do you want to get a hot drink before we hit the road?'

'No, let's head off straight away.'

The names of the towns and villages flashed by once more in the glare of the headlights, but this time in reverse order, like a film being rewound. Sometimes, at the youth club, Gabriel used to help the priest pack away the projection equipment. It was magical to see Charlie Chaplin step backwards onto a roof from which he had fallen only fifteen minutes earlier. Of course it was a film, but in his heart of hearts Gabriel thought it possible to do something similar in real life: to crank back the camera and, hey presto, wipe the slate clean and start again.

'Gabriel, you know, I think I'm going to take your advice.'

'What do you mean?'

'Go to an island in the sun. I'm going to find a job in a little hotel and perhaps, maybe, a husband. And I'm going to spend my days swimming, not thinking of anything.'

'That's a very good idea, Madeleine.'

Yes, I think so too. Can you stop at that service station? I want a coffee. Could you go and get me one?'

'Of course.'

A gust of wind blew into the car as Gabriel opened the door. It was as if someone was pushing from the other side, preventing him from getting out.

'Would you like sugar?'

'Yes, please.'

Just before he stepped out Madeleine grasped his hand.

'Gabriel?'

'Yes?'

'Thank you.'

An elderly woman was having trouble with the vending machine. Her feeble fingers pressed all the buttons in vain.

'Would you like me to try?'

With the palm of his hand Gabriel hit the side of the machine, which immediately delivered a cup and jerkily filled it with brownish liquid.

'Thank you, you're very kind.'

'My pleasure.'

Using the same method, Gabriel filled his own soft plastic cup with the same indiscriminate liquid.

Outside, the car was gone. In its place lay his bag, abandoned on the asphalt. There were only three or four cars parked on the forecourt and José's car wasn't one of them. Gabriel immediately realised what had happened. Madeleine was a good woman. She had done what she had to do. He picked up his bag, threw the cup in a bin and crossed the forecourt.

The harsh neon light created petrol rainbows in the iridescent shimmering puddles of water. There was no need to look up at the sky to admire the stars. They were all there, fallen on the ground. You could walk on them and splash them. A car engine growled. It was a small Austin. It looked like a toy car. Gabriel knocked on the window.

'Excuse me, madame, but would you mind giving me a lift to the nearest train station?'

'I'm going to Morlaix. Ah, you're the one who helped with the coffee machine. Come on, get in.'

The car was small, no bigger than a family-size box of matches. With his bag on his knees Gabriel climbed in as best he could. It smelt of mints.

'Thank you very much.'

'I don't normally take hitchhikers, but seeing as you helped me with the coffee machine it's the least I can do. We already know each other a bit. And, anyway, Morlaix isn't far. You wouldn't have the time to do away with me!'

The woman gave a tinkling laugh. Gabriel's laugh was a little forced. The woman drove in fits and starts with her nose up close to the steering wheel and her forehead almost touching the front windscreen.

'You know, I complained at the checkout about their coffee machine, but they didn't care! And I followed all the instructions properly!'

'I'm sure you did.'

'I'll tell you something. I don't for a moment believe in their progress. It's like the telephone. My children bought me a mobile phone because it reassures them. Well, believe it or not, the thing doesn't work. And it's always my fault. I'm never in the right place, or I didn't recharge the batteries, or I pressed the wrong button, goodness knows what else! There's always something that makes it my fault. They bought me a computer as well, to be closer to me, apparently. And so now I only see my grandchildren in photos and I don't get postcards any more. It's a young person's world, full of buttons. That's how it is. Anyway, no offence, but aren't you a bit too old to be hitchhiking?'

'It's a long story. I was supposed to meet somebody.'

'Where are you heading?'

'The south.'

'The south is a good place to grow old. Cannes is nice. What on earth is going on up ahead?'

A maelstrom of flashing blue lights filled the sky as a policeman dressed in a fluorescent jacket signalled to the oncoming cars to slow down. Driving up to him, the woman wound down her window.

'What's going on?'

'There's been an accident.'

'Is it serious?'

'Someone's been killed. A woman. If she had wanted to kill herself, she couldn't have done a better job. It's a straight road. Either that or she fell asleep at the wheel. Could you move on, please? There are people behind you.'

José's car sat smoking, crumpled up against a wall as firemen in shiny helmets covered it in dry ice.

'People drive like idiots. They drive at top speed and to go where?'

'To an island.'

'Sorry?'

'Nothing, I was just saying.'

The railway platform was deserted. Above him, a tangle of metal girders merged into the gloom.

Pascal Garnier In His
Own Words

Pascal Garnier, who died in March 2010, was a talented novelist, short story writer, children's author and painter. From his home in the mountains of the Ardèche, he wrote fiction in a noir palette with a cast of characters drawn from ordinary provincial life. Though his writing is often very dark in tone, it sparkles with quirkily beautiful imagery and dry wit. Garnier's work has been likened to the great thriller writer, Georges Simenon.

Gallic Books will publish three novels by Pascal Garnier in 2012: The Panda Theory, How's the Pain? and The A26.

In an article for his French publisher, Zulma, Garnier described what led him to become a writer:

According to my birth certificate, I was born on 4th July 1949 in the 14th arrondissement of Paris. I can't say I remember the event, but let's assume that's how it happened. Afterwards came a normal childhood in what you'd call the average French family - which felt more and more average the more it dawned on me that

I'd been sold a world with no user's manual, lured in by false advertising. When I was about fifteen, the state education system and I agreed to go our separate ways. I'd had enough, I was suffocating, convinced that real life was going on somewhere else. So off I went in search of it. In those days you could still travel freely through North Africa, the Middle and Far East. With my head in the clouds, I roamed about for a decade or so until I came to see that it really is a very small world and, being round, you always end up back where you started.

That's when the wife and baby came along. All around me, the faithful companions I'd met along the way were nestling back into their kennels, burying their dreams and delusions like bones to gnaw at in years to come when they were old and toothless. Rebelling against such mass surrender, I threw myself into rock and roll – and landed with a resounding thud. I was no better at being a pop star than I was at being a dad. Still, it was writing my pitiful ditties that gave me a taste for words. Deep down, I harboured a wild dream of writing something longer, something like a book. But my limited vocabulary, terrible spelling and hopeless grammar seemed like insurmountable obstacles. So I got divorced, remarried, dabbled in design for women's magazines, took on odd jobs, got up to the occasional bit of mischief. In short, I was killing time, frittering my life away. The boredom of my childhood numbed me once again with the sweetness of a drug. I was thirty-five.

You can only escape if you're imprisoned, which to some extent I was. I had no choice: my only way out was through a blank page. Slowly scraping along, I dug myself out through a corner of the kitchen table, and as I tunnelled my way up to the surface, I filled the hole within myself. One short story, then two, then three... And then one day I had a publisher on the phone, and not just any publisher, but POL. A collection of twelve short stories was published under the title 'L'année sabbatique', 'A year's sabbatical'. After that, another sixty-odd books were brought out by several other publishers: books for children, books for adults, books labelled as noir or white, whatever - I've never been interested in that particular apartheid. So there it is, a bit muddled I'll admit. I write because, as Pessoa said: 'Literature is proof that life is not enough'.

Pascal Garnier
How's the Pain?

Death is Simon's business. And now the ageing vermin exterminator is preparing to die. But he still has one last job down on the coast and he needs a driver.

Bernard is twenty-one. He can drive and he's never seen the sea. He can't pass up the chance to chauffeur for Simon, whatever his mother may say.

As the unlikely pair set off on their journey, Bernard soon finds that Simon's definition of vermin is broader than he'd expected...

Veering from the hilarious to the horrific, this offbeat story from master stylist, Pascal Garnier, is at heart an affecting study of human frailty.

ISBN 978-1-9083-1303-4
Published June 2012
£6.99